CH

GAY-NECK
The Story of a Pigeon

Also by Dhan Gopal Mukerji

GHOND The Hunter
HARI The Jungle Lad
KARI The Elephant

GAY-NECK
The Story of a Pigeon

by Dhan Gopal Mukerji

Illustrated by
Boris Artzybasheff

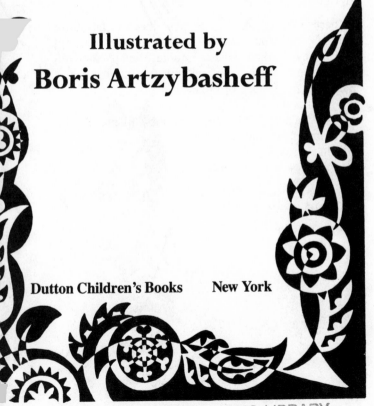

Dutton Children's Books   New York

Published in the United States by Dutton Children's Books, a division of Penguin USA
375 Hudson Street
New York, New York 10014

Library of Congress Catalog Card Number: 68-13419
ISBN: 0-525-30400-2

30 29 28 27 26 25 24 23 22

To
Suresh Chandra Banerji, Esq.

DEAR SURESCH:

Since *Gay-Neck* needs a protector, I thought of you for several reasons. First of all, being a poet, an observer of nature, and a traveller, you would be able to protect the book from being condemned. In fact, there is no one who can do it as well as yourself.

You know the country where Gay-Neck grew. You are versed in the lore of birds. For a pigeon, life is a repetition of two incidents: namely, quest of food and avoidance of attacks by its enemies. If the hero of the present book repeats his escapes from attacks by hawks, it is because that is the sort of mishap that becomes chronic in the case of pigeons.

Now as to my sources, you well know that they are too numerous to be mentioned here. Many hunters, poets like yourself, and books in many languages have helped me to write *Gay-Neck*. And if you will permit it, I hope to discharge at least a part of my debt by dedicating this book to one of my sources—yourself.

I remain most faithfully yours,
DHAN GOPAL

Contents

List of Illustrations

PART ONE

Birth of Gay-Neck

THE CITY OF CAL-cutta, which boasts of a million people, must have at least two million pigeons. Every third Hindu boy has perhaps a dozen pet carriers, tumblers, fan-tails and pouters. The art of domesticating pigeons goes back thousands of years in India, and she has contributed two species of pigeons as a special product of her bird fanciers, the fan-tail and the pouter. Love and care have been showered on pigeons for centuries by emperors, princes and queens in their marble palaces, as well as by the poor, in their humble homes. The gardens, grottos and fountains of the Indian rich—the small field of flowers and fruits of the common folk, each has its orna-

ment and music—many-coloured pigeons and cooing white doves with ruby eyes.

Even now, any winter morning, foreigners who
visit our big cities may see on the flat-roofed houses
innumerable boys waving white flags as signals to
their pet pigeons flying up in the crisp cold air.
Through the blue heavens flocks of the birds soar
like vast clouds. They start in small flocks, and
spend about twenty minutes circling over the roofs
of their owners' homes. Then they slowly ascend,
and all the separate groups from different houses of
the town merge into one big flock, and float far out
of sight. How they ever return to their own homes
is a wonder, for all the house-tops look alike in
shape in spite of their rose, yellow, violet and white
colours.

But pigeons have an amazing sense of direction
and love of their owners. I have yet to see creatures more loyal than pigeons and elephants. I have
played with both, and the tusker on four feet in the
country, or the bird on two wings in the city, no
matter how far they wandered, were by their almost
infallible instinct brought back to their friend and
brother—Man.

My elephant friend was called Kari, of whom
you have heard before, and the other pet that I
knew well was a pigeon. His name was Chitra-griva;
Chitra meaning "painted in gay colours," and Griva,
"neck"—in one phrase, pigeon Gay-Neck. Sometimes he was called "Iridescence-throated."

Of course, Gay-Neck did not come out of his egg with an iridescent throat; he had to grow the feathers week by week; and until he was three months old, there was very little hope that he would acquire the brilliant collar; but at last, when he did achieve it, he was the most beautiful pigeon in my town in India, and the boys of my town owned forty thousand pigeons.

But I must begin this story at the very beginning, I mean with Gay-Neck's parents. His father was a tumbler who married the most beautiful pigeon of his day; she came from a noble old stock of carriers. That is why Gay-Neck proved himself later such a worthy carrier pigeon in war as well as in peace. From his mother he inherited wisdom, from his father bravery and alertness. He was so quick-witted that sometimes he escaped the clutches of a hawk by tumbling at the last moment right over the enemy's head. But of that later, in its proper time and place.

Now let me tell you what a narrow escape Gay-Neck had while still in the egg. I shall never forget the day when, through a mistake of mine, I broke one of the two eggs that his mother had laid. It was very stupid of me. I regret it even now. Who knows? Maybe with that broken egg perished the finest pigeon of the world. It happened in this way. Our house was four stories high—and on its roof was built our pigeon-house. A few days after the eggs were laid I decided to clean the pigeon-hole in which Gay-Neck's mother was sitting on them. I lifted her gently and put her on the roof beside me. Then I lifted each egg carefully and put it most softly in the next pigeon-hole, which, however, had no cotton or flannel on its hard wooden floor. Then I busied myself with the task of removing the debris from the birth-nest. As soon as that was done, I brought one egg back and restored it to its proper place. Next I reached for the second one and laid a gentle but firm hand on it. Just then something fell upon my face like a roof blown by the storm. It was Gay-Neck's father furiously beating my face with his wings. Worse still, he had placed the claws of one of his feet on my nose. The pain and surprise of it was so great that ere I knew how, I had dropped the egg. I was engrossed in beating off the bird from my head and face, and at last he flew away. But too late: the little egg lay broken in a mess at my feet. I was furious with its clumsy father and also with myself. Why with myself? Because I should have been prepared for the father bird's attack. He took me for a stealer of his eggs, and in his ignorance was risking his life to prevent my robbing his nest. May I impress it upon you that you should antici-pate all kinds of surprise attacks when cleaning a bird's home during nesting season.

But to go on with our story. The mother bird knew the day when she was to break open the egg-shell with her own beak, in order to usher Gay-Neck into the world. Though the male sits on the egg pretty nearly one-third of the time—for he does that each day from morning till late afternoon—yet he does not know when the hour of his child's birth is at hand. No one save the mother bird arrives at that divine certainty. We do not yet understand the nature of the unique wireless message by which she learns that within the shell the yolk and the white of her egg have turned into a baby-bird. She also knows how to tap the right spot so that the shell will break open without injuring her child in the slightest. To me that is as good as a miracle.

Gay-Neck's birth happened exactly as I have described. About the twentieth day after the laying of the egg, I noticed that the mother was not sitting on it any more. She pecked the father and drove him away every time he flew down from the roof of the house and volunteered to sit on the egg. Then he cooed, which meant, "Why do you send me away?"

She, the mother, just pecked him the more, meaning, "Please go. The business on hand is very serious."

At that, the father flew away. That worried me, for I was anxious for the egg to hatch, and was feeling suspicious about its doing it at all. With increased interest and anxiety I watched the pigeonhole. An hour passed. Nothing happened. It was about the third quarter of the next hour that the mother turned her head one way and listened to something—probably a stirring inside that egg.

Then she gave a slight start. I felt as if a tremor were running through her whole body. With it a great resolution came into her. Now she raised her head, and took aim. In two strokes she cracked the egg open, revealing a wee bird, all beak and a tiny shivering body! Now watch the mother. She is surprised. Was it this that she was expecting all these long days? Oh, how small, how helpless! The moment she realizes her child's helplessness, she covers him up with the soft blue feathers of her breast.

Education of Gay-Neck

THERE ARE TWO sweet sights in the bird world: one when the mother breaks open her egg in order to bring to light her child, and the other when she broods and feeds him. Gay-Neck was brooded most affectionately by both his parents. This brooding did for him what cuddling does for human children. It gives the helpless ones warmth and happiness. It is as necessary to them as food. This is the time when a pigeon-hole should not be stuffed with too much cotton or flannel, which should be put there more and more sparingly so that the temperature of the nest does not get too hot. Ignorant pigeon fanciers do not realize that as the baby grows larger he puts forth more and more heat from his own body. And I think it is wise not to clean the nest frequently during this time. Everything that the parents allow to remain in the nest contributes to making their baby comfortable and happy.

I remember distinctly how, from the second day of his birth, little Gay-Neck automatically opened his beak and expanded his carnation-coloured body like a bellows every time one of his parents flew back to their nest. The father or the mother put their beaks into his wide-open maw and poured into it the milk made in their own organs from millet seeds that they had eaten. I noticed this; the food that was poured into his mouth was very soft. No pigeon ever gives any seeds to its baby even when it is nearly a month old without first keeping them in its throat for some time, which softens the food before it enters the delicate stomach of the baby.

Our Gay-Neck was a tremendous eater. He kept one of his parents busy getting food while the other brooded or stayed with him. I think the father bird brooded and worked for him no less hard than the mother. No wonder his body grew very fat. His carnation colour changed into a yellowish-white— the first sign of feathers coming on. Then that gave way to prickly white feathers, round and somewhat stiff, like a porcupine needle. The yellow things that hung about his mouth and eyes fell away. Slowly the beak emerged, firm, sharp and long. What a powerful jaw! When he was about three weeks old, an ant was crawling past him into the pigeon-hole at whose entrance he was sitting. Without any instruction from anybody he struck it with his beak. Where there had been a whole ant now lay its two halves. He brought his nose down to the dead ant and examined what he had done. There was no doubt that he had taken that black ant for a seed, and killed an innocent passer-by who was friendly to his race. Let us hope he was ashamed of it. Anyway, he never killed another ant the rest of his life.

By the time he was five weeks old he could hop out of his birth-nest and take a drink from the pan of water left near the pigeon-holes. Even now he had to be fed by his parents, though every day he tried to get food on his own account. He would sit on my wrist and dig up a seed at a time from the palm of my hand. He juggled it two or three times in his throat like a juggler throwing up balls in the air, and swallowed it. Every time Gay-Neck did that, he turned his head and looked into my eyes as much as to say: "Am I not doing it well? You must tell my parents how clever I am when they come down from sunning themselves on the roof." All the same, he was the slowest of my pigeons in developing his powers.

Just at this time I made a discovery. I never knew before how pigeons could fly in a dust-storm without going blind. But as I watched the ever-growing Gay-Neck, I noticed one day that a film was drawn over his eyes. I thought he was losing his sight. In my consternation I put forth my hand to draw him nearer to my face in order to examine him closely. No sooner had I made the gesture than he opened his golden eyes and receded into the rear of the hole. But just the same I caught him and took him up on the roof, and in the burning sunlight of May I scrutinized his eyelids. Yes, there it was: he had, attached to his eyelid, another thin lid as delicate as tissue-paper, and every time I put his face toward the sun he drew that film over the two orbits of gold. And so I learned that it was a protective film for the eye that enabled the bird to fly in a dust-storm or straight toward the sun.

In another fortnight Gay-Neck was taught how to fly. It was not at all easy, bird though he was by birth. A human child may love the water, yet he has to make mistakes and swallow water while learning the art of swimming. Similarly with my pigeon. He had a mild distrust of opening his wings, and for hours he sat on our roof, where the winds of the sky blew without quickening him to flight. In order to make the situation clear, let me describe our roof to you. It was railed with a solid concrete wall as high as a boy of fourteen. That prevented even a sleep-walker from slipping off the height of four stories on summer nights, when most of us slept on the roof.

Gay-Neck I put on that concrete wall every day. There he sat for hours at a time, facing the wind, but that was all. One day I put some peanuts on the roof and called him to hop down and get them. He looked at me with an inquiring eye for a few moments. Turning from me, he looked down again at the peanuts. He repeated this process several times. When at last he was convinced that I was not going to bring these delicious morsels up for him to eat, he began to walk up and down the railing, craning his neck occasionally towards the peanuts about three feet below. At last, after fifteen minutes of heart-breaking hesitancy, he hopped down. Just as his feet struck the floor, his wings, hitherto unopened, suddenly spread themselves out full sail as he balanced himself over the nuts. What a triumph!

About this time I noticed the change of colours on his feathers. Instead of a nondescript grey-blue, a glossy aquamarine glowed all over him. And suddenly one morning in the sunlight his throat glistened like iridescent beads.

Now came the supreme question of flight. I waited for his parents to teach him the first lessons, though I helped the only way I could. Every day for a few minutes I made him perch on my wrist; then I would swing my arm up and down many times, and in order to balance himself on such a difficult perch he had to shut and open his wings frequently. That was good for him, but there ended my part of the teaching. You may ask me the rea-

son of my hurrying matters so. He was already behind in his flying lessons, and in June the rains begin
to fall in India; and with the approach of the rainy
season any long flight becomes impossible. I wished
to train him in learning his directions as soon as I
could.

However, one day long before the end of May,
his father undertook the task. This particular day a
brisk north wind, which had been sweeping about
and cooling the atmosphere of the city, had just
died down. The sky was as clear as a limpid sapphire. The spaces were so clear that you could see
the house-tops of our town, then the fields and ar-
bours of the country in the farthest distance. About
three o'clock in the afternoon, Gay-Neck was sunning himself on the concrete wall of the roof. His
father, who had been flying about in the air, came
down and perched next to him. He looked at his
son with a queer glance, as much as to say: "Here,
lazy-bones, you are nearly three months old, yet you
do not dare to fly. Are you a pigeon or an earth-
worm?" But Gay-Neck, the soul of dignity, made
no answer. That exasperated his father, who began
to coo and boom at him in pigeon-language. In
order to get away from that volubility, Gay-Neck
moved; but his father followed, cooing, booming
and banging his wings. Gay-Neck went on removing
himself farther and farther; and the old fellow, instead of relenting, redoubled his talk, and pursued.

At last the father pushed him so close to the edge
that Gay-Neck had only one alternative, that is, to
slip off the roof. Suddenly his father thrust upon his
young body all the weight of his old frame. Gay-
Neck slipped. Hardly had he fallen half a foot when
he opened his wings, and flew. Oh, what an exhilarating moment for all concerned! His mother, who
was downstairs dipping herself in the water, and
performing her afternoon toilet, came up through
the staircase and flew to keep her son company.
They circled above the roof for at least ten minutes
before they came down to perch. When they reached
the roof the mother folded her wings as a matter of
course, and sat still. Not so the son: he was in a
panic, like a boy walking into cold and deep water.
His whole body shook, and his feet trod the roof
gingerly as he alighted, skating over it furiously and
flapping his wings in order to balance himself. At
last he stopped, as his chest struck the side of the
wall, and he folded his wings as swiftly as we shut a
fan. Gay-Neck was panting with excitement, while
his mother rubbed him and placed her chest against
him as if he were a mere baby who badly needed
brooding. Seeing that his task had been done suc-
cessfully, Gay-Neck's father went down to take his
bath.

Training in Direction

NOW THAT, LIKE A newly trained diver, he had overcome his fear of plunging into the air, Gay-Neck ventured on longer and higher flights. In a week's time he was able to fly steadily for half an hour, and when he came home to the roof, he swooped down as gracefully as his parents. There was no more of that panicky beating of wings in order to balance himself as his feet touched the roof.

His parents, who had accompanied Gay-Neck in his preliminary flights, now began to leave him behind, and to fly much higher above him. For a while I thought that they were trying to make him fly still higher; for the son always made an effort to reach

the level of his parents. Perhaps his elders were
setting the little fellow a superb example. But at last,
one day early in June, that explanation of mine was
shaken by the following fateful incident. Gay-Neck
was flying high: he looked half his usual size. Above
him flew his parents, almost as small as a man's fist.
They were circling above him with the regularity
of a merry-go-round. It looked monotonous and
meaningless. I removed my gaze from them; after
all, it is not comfortable to look steadily upwards
for long. As I lowered my eyes towards the horizon,
they were held by a black spot moving swiftly, and
growing larger every second. I wondered what sort
of bird he was, coming at such a speed in a straight
line, for in India birds are named in the Sanskrit,
Turyak, or "curve-tracers."

But this one was coming straight, like an arrow.
In another two minutes my doubts were dispelled.
It was a hawk making for little Gay-Neck. I looked
up and beheld a miraculous sight. His father was
tumbling steadily down in order to reach his level,
while his mother, bent on the same purpose, was
making swift downward curves. Ere the terrible
hawk had come within ten yards of the innocent
little fellow, both his flanks were covered. Now the
three flew downwards at a right angle from the path
of their enemy. Undeterred by such a move, the
hawk charged. At once the three pigeons made a
dip that frustrated him, but the force with which

he had made the attack was so great that it carried
him a long distance beyond them. The pigeons kept
on circling in the air with an ever-increasing downward trend. In another minute they were half-way
to our roof. Now the hawk changed his mind. He
went higher and higher into the sky: in fact, he
flew so high that the pigeons could not hear the
wind whistling in the feathers of his wings; and as
he was above them they could not see their foe.
Feeling that they were safe, they relaxed. It was evi-
dent that they were not flying so fast as before. Just
then I saw that above them, way up, the hawk was
folding his wings: he was about to drop, and in an
instant he fell upon them like a stone. In despera-
tion I put my fingers in my mouth and made a shrill
whistle, a cry of warning. The pigeons dived like
a falling sword, yet the hawk followed. Inch by
inch, moment by moment he was gaining on them.
Faster and faster he fell: now there were scarcely
twenty feet between him and his prey. There was
no doubt that he was aiming at Gay-Neck. I could
see his sinister claws. "Won't those stupid pigeons
do anything to save themselves?" I thought in an
agony. He was so near him now—if they would only
keep their heads, and— Just then they made a vast
upward circle. The hawk followed. Then they flew
on an even but large elliptical path. If a bird flies
in a circle, he either tends to swing to the centre of
that circle or away from it. Now the hawk missed

their intention, and tended towards the centre, making a small circle inside their big one. No sooner was his back turned to them than the three pigeons made another dive, almost to our roof, but the sinister one was not to be deterred. He followed like a tongue of black lightning. His prey made a curving dive onto the roof, where they were safe at last under my wide-spread arms! That instant I heard the shriek of the wind in the air; about a foot above my head the hawk flew by, his eyes blazing with yellow fire and his claws quivering like the tongue of a viper. As he passed I could hear the wind still whistling in his feathers.

After that narrow escape of my pet birds, I began to train Gay-Neck to a sense of direction. One day I took all three birds in a cage towards the east of our town. Exactly at nine in the morning I set them free. They came home safely. The next day I took them an equal distance to the west. Inside a week they knew the way to our house from within a radius of at least fifteen miles in any direction.

Since nothing ends smoothly in this world, the training of Gay-Neck finally met with a check. I had taken him and his parents down the Ganges in a boat. When we started, it was about six in the morning. The sky was littered with stray clouds, and a moderate wind was blowing from the south. Our boat was piled high with rice as white as snow on whose top were heaped mangoes red and golden in colour, like a white peak afire with the sunset.

I should have foreseen that such auspicious weather might turn suddenly into a terrible storm, for after all, boy though I was, I knew something about the freaks of the monsoon in June.

Hardly had we gone twenty miles before the first rain-clouds of the season raced across the sky. The velocity of the wind was so great that it ripped off one of the sails of our boat. Seeing that there was no time to be lost, I opened the cage and released the three pigeons. As they struck the wind, they vaulted right over and flew very low, almost falling into the water. They flew thus close to the surface of the river for a quarter of an hour, making very little headway against the hard wind. But they persisted, and another ten minutes saw them safely tacking and flying landward. Just about the time they had reached the string of villages on our left, the sky grew pitch black, a torrential cloudburst blotted everything out, and we saw nothing but inky sheets of water through which the lightning zig-zagged and danced the dance of death. I gave up all hope of finding my pigeons again. We were almost shipwrecked ourselves, but fortunately our boat was beached on the shore of a village. Next morning, when I came home by train, I found two wet pigeons instead of three. Gay-Neck's father had perished in the storm. No doubt it was all my fault; and for the few days that followed, our house was given up to mourning. The two pigeons and I used to go up on the roof, whenever the rain left off a bit, in order to scan the sky for a glimpse of the father. Alas, he never returned.

Gay-Neck in the Himalayas

SINCE THE RAIN AND the heat in the plains proved excessive, my family decided to take us to the Himalayas. If you take a map of India, you will find that in its northeast corner is a town called Darjeeling, standing almost face to face with Mount Everest, the highest peak in the world. After travelling, not too fast, by caravan, several days from Darjeeling, my family, myself and my two pigeons reached the little village of Dentam. There we were ten thousand feet above sea-level. At such a height an American mountain or the Alps would have at least some snow, but in India, which is in the tropics, and on the Himalayas, hardly thirty degrees north of the equator, the snow-line does not commence under ten thousand feet, and the jungle of the foot-hills, abounding with animals, is so cold after September that all its denizens migrate southwards.

Let me give you just a slight picture of our setting. Our house of stone and mud overlooked small valleys where tea was grown. Beyond, between serried ridges that stuck out in harsh but majestic curves, were valleys full of rice-fields, maize, and fruit orchards. Farther on rose the dark evergreen-clad precipices over which reared thousands of feet of pure white ranges, the Kangchenjunga, the peak Makalu, and the Everest ranges. In the first flush of dawn they looked white; but as the light grew in brightness and the sun rose higher, peak after peak defined itself, not far off on the horizon, but piercing the very middle of the sky whence poured a flood of crimson light like the very blood of benediction.

One usually sees the Himalayas best in the early morning, for they are covered with clouds during the rest of the day. Hindus, who are religious people, get up in good time to behold the sublime hills and to pray to God. Can there be a better setting to prayers than those mountains most of whose peaks yet remain unexplored and untrodden by man? Their inviolate sanctity is something precious that remains a perpetual symbol of divinity. Heights like that of the Everest are symbols of the highest reality—GOD. They are symbolic of God's mystery, too, for with the exception of the early morning they are, as I have said, shrouded with clouds all day. Foreigners who come to India imagine they would like to see them all the time; but let no one complain, for he who has beheld Everest in its morning grandeur and awe-inspiring glory will say: "It is too sublime to be gazed at all day long. None could bear it continually before his eyes."

In July those early-morning views of the Everest are not vouchsafed us every day, for it is the month of rain. All the ranges lie in the grip of the most devastating blizzards. Once in a while, above the battle of storms and driven snow, the peaks appear —a compact mass of hard ice and white fire. They glow intensely in the sunlight, while at their feet the snow-clouds whirl and fall like fanatical dervishes dancing frenziedly before their terrible god.

During the summer my friend Radja and our teacher in jungle lore, old Ghond, came to visit our home. Radja was about sixteen years old, already a Brahmin priest, and Ghond we always called old, for none knew his age. Both Radja and I were handed over to that most competent of hunters for the purpose of studying under his guidance the secrets of jungle and animal life. Since I have described them in my other books, I need not repeat myself here.

As soon as we had settled down in Dentam, I began to train my pigeons in the art of direction.

Whenever we had a clear day we climbed all the forenoon toward the higher peaks amid ilexes and balsam forests, and released our birds from some monastery roof or from the house of a nobleman. And towards evening, when we returned home, we invariably found Gay-Neck and his mother there before us.

We had hardly half a dozen clear days during the whole month of July, but under the guidance of the almost omniscient Ghond, and with my friend Radja, we travelled very far in a short time. We visited and stayed with all classes of the mountain folk, who looked much like Chinese. Their manners were elegant and their hospitality was generous. Of course, we took the pigeons with us, sometimes in a cage but most of the time under our tunics. Though we were frequently soaked with rain, Gay-Neck and his mother were religiously guarded from the weather.

Towards the end of July we made a journey beyond every lamasery (monastery) and baron's castle of Sikkim that we three human beings and the two pigeons had seen and known. We passed Singalila, where there was a nice little lamasery, on towards Phalut and the Unknown. At last we reached the homeland of the eagles. Around us were bare granite cliffs surrounded by fir trees and stunted pines; before us to the north lay the Kangchenjunga and the Everest ranges. Here, on the edge of an abyss, we released our two birds. In that exhilarating air they flew like children running from school at the end of the day. Gay-Neck's mother flew far upwards in order to show her son the sublime heights.

After the two birds had flown away, we three men talked of what they might be seeing as they sped above the altitudes. Before them, no doubt, rose the twin peaks of the Kangchenjunga group, slightly lower than Mount Everest but just as impeccable and austere as that immaculate peak untrodden still by the feet of men. That fact roused profound emotions in us. We saw the mountain in the distance, just for a few minutes, like a mirror before the Face of God, and I said to myself: "O thou summit of sanctity, thou inviolate and eternal, may no man tarnish thee, nor may any mortal stain thy purity even by his slightest touch. May thou remain forever unvanquished, O thou backbone of the universe, and measurement of immortality."

But I have brought you so high not to tell you about mountains, but of an adventure that befell us there. Now that Gay-Neck and his mother had flown, we gave up watching them and went in quest of an eagle's nest that was on a neighbouring cliff. The Himalayan eagle is brown with a soft golden glow, and though very beautiful to look at—it is in perfect proportion of beauty with strength—yet it is a fierce beast of prey.

But at first on this particular afternoon we encountered nothing savage. On the contrary, we found two fluffy white eaglets in an eyrie. They looked as engaging as new-born babes. The southern wind was blowing right in their eyes, but they did not mind it. It is in the nature of the Himalayan eagle to build his nest facing the direction of the wind. Why? No one knows. Apparently the bird likes to face that which he floats up on.

The younglings were nearly three weeks old, for they were already shedding their birthday cotton-like appearance, and had begun to grow real plumage. Their talons were sharp enough for their age, and their beaks hard and keen.

An eagle's eyrie is open and large. Its entrance-ledge—that is to say, landing-place—is about six or seven feet wide, and quite clean. But within, where it is dark and narrow, there is a perfect litter of twigs, branches, and a little of the hair and feathers of victims, every other part of their prey being devoured by the eaglets. The parents devour most of the bones, hair and feathers with the meat.

Though the surrounding country was clad in stunted pine trees, yet it was full of bird noises. Also, strange insects buzzed in the fir trees. Jewelled flies fluttered on blue wings over mauve orchids, and enormous rhododendrons glowed in sizes sometimes as large as the moon. Now and then a wild cat called, apparently talking in his noonday sleep.

Suddenly Ghond told us to run a dozen yards and hide in a bush. Hardly had we done so when the noises about us began to subside. In another sixty seconds the insects stopped their buzzing, the birds ceased to call, and even the trees seemed to grow still with expectation. In the air slowly rose the thin whistle of something. In a few moments it fell into a lower key. Hard upon it came a weird noise almost sounding like a shriek, and a giant bird flew down to the eagle's eyrie. The wind was still whistling in its wings. By its size Ghond thought it was the mother of the two babies. She remained still in the air till the eaglets withdrew into the inner recesses of their home. From her talons hung something well skinned, like a large rabbit. She landed, dropping her prey on the ledge. One could see that her wings from tip to tip measured half a dozen feet. She folded them as a man folds a paper; then, seeing that her children were coming towards her, she drew in her talons lest they pierce their unarmoured tender flesh. Now she hobbled like a cripple. The two little fellows ran and disappeared under her half-open wings, but they did not want to be brooded, for they were hungry. So she led them outwards to the dead rabbit, tore away some of its flesh, excluded any bone that clung to it, and gave it to them to swallow. Again, from below and all about, the insects and birds resumed their noises. We rose from our hiding and started homeward after Radja and I had extracted a promise from Ghond that he would bring us back later to see the full-fledged eaglets.

And so in a little over a month we returned. We brought with us Gay-Neck and his mother, for I wished the little fellow to fly the second time so that he would know with absolute certainty every village, lamasery, lake and river as well as the beasts, and the other birds—cranes, parrots, Himalayan herons, wild geese, divers, sparrow-hawks and swifts. On this trip we went about a hundred yards beyond the eagle's nest. The finger of autumn had already touched the rhododendrons. Their flaming petals were falling out; their long stems, many feet high, rustled in the winds. Leaves of many trees had begun to turn, and the air was full of melancholy. At about eleven, we uncaged our pigeons, who flew away into the sapphire sky that hung like a sail from the white peaks.

They had flown for about half an hour when a hawk appeared above them. It drew nearer the two pigeons and then drove at them. But the prey proved too wary; they escaped scatheless. Just as Gay-Neck and his mother were coming down swiftly to where the trees were, the hawk's mate appeared and attacked. She flew at them as her husband had done, without gaining her objective. Seeing that their prey was escaping, the male hawk cried shrilly to his mate; at that, she stopped in the air, just marking time. The pigeons, feeling safe, quickened their wing motion and flew southwards, while the two hawks followed, converging upon them from the east and the west. Wing-beat upon wing-beat, they gained on the pigeons. Their wings, shaped like a butcher's hatchet tipped off at the end, cut through the air like a storm . . . one, two, three— they fell like spears! Gay-Neck's mother stopped, and just floated in the air. That upset the calculation of the hawks. What to do now? Which one to fall upon? Such questioning takes time, and Gay-Neck seized the chance to change his course. Swiftly he rose higher and higher. In a few moments his example was followed by his mother, but she had lost time, and the hawks rose almost vaulting up to her. Then apparently a sudden panic seized her; she was afraid that the hawks were after her son, and in order to protect him—which was utterly unnecessary—she flew towards the two pursuers. In another minute both of those birds of prey had pounced upon her. The air was filled with a shower of feathers! The sight frightened Gay-Neck, who fell upon the nearest cliff for protection and safety. It was his mother's error that deprived her of her own life and probably imperiled that of her son.

We three human beings began a search for the cliff where Gay-Neck had fallen. It was no easy task, for the Himalayas are very treacherous. Pythons, if not tigers, were to be feared. Yet my friend

Radja insisted, and Ghond the hunter agreed with him, saying that it would augment our knowledge.

We descended from the cliff that we were on and entered a narrow gorge where the raw bones lying on the ground convinced us that some beast of prey had dined on its victim the previous night. But we were not frightened, for our leader was Ghond, the most well-equipped hunter of Bengal. Very soon we began a laborious climb through clefts and crevices full of purple orchids on green moss. The odour of fir and balsam filled our nostrils. Sometimes we saw a rhododendron still in bloom. The air was cold and the climb unending. After two in the afternoon, having lunched on a handful of chola (dried beans softened in water), we reached the cliff where Gay-Neck was hiding. To our surprise we discovered that it was the eagle's nest with two eaglets—the babies of our previous visit—now full-fledged. They were sitting on the front ledge of their eyrie, while to our utter amazement we saw Gay-Neck at the farthest corner of a neighbouring ledge, cowering and weak. At out approach the eaglets came forward to attack us with their beaks. Radja, whose hand was nearest, received an awful stroke that ripped open the skin of his thumb, whence blood flowed freely. The eagles were between us and Gay-Neck, and there was nothing to be done but to climb over a higher cliff to reach him. Hardly had we gone six yards away from the nest when Ghond signed to us to hide as we had done the first time we had come. We did so with celerity, under a pine, and soon, with a soft roar in the air, one of the parent eagles drew near. In a few seconds there fell a high-pitched sound as the eagle sailed into its nest. A shiver of exquisite pleasure ran up and down my spine as her tail-feather grazed our tree and I heard that whistling mute itself.

Let me re-emphasize the fact that people who have an idea that the eagle builds its nest on an isolated, inaccessible cliff are mistaken. A powerful bird or beast does not have to be so careful in choosing its home. It can afford to be negligent. The nest of such a gigantic bird must have as its first requirement space so that it can open and shut its wings in the outer court of its home, and a place so spacious cannot be too inaccessible. Next, the eagle has no knack at building nests. It chooses a ledge that juts out of a cliff-cavern where nature has already performed two-thirds of the task. The last third is done by the birds themselves, and it merely consists in getting branches, leaves, and blades of grass together as a rough bed where the eggs may be laid and hatched.

All those details we gathered as we crawled out of our hiding-place and examined—for the second time—the eyrie from a distance. There was no doubt that they were our old friends—the two babies—grown big, and their mother. She, even now though they were grown up, drew in her talons as a matter of habit lest they hurt her children. But it was momentary; after she had made sure that they were racing to meet her, she opened them and stood firmly on the outer ledge. The eaglets, though they should not be called so now that they were full-fledged, rushed forward and took shelter under her wide-spread wings. But the little beasts did not stay there long; they did not want to be loved; they were very hungry; they wanted something to eat, and alas, she had brought nothing. At that, they turned from her and sat facing the wind, waiting.

At Ghond's signal we all three rose and began to climb. In the course of another hour we had crawled in lizard-like silence over the roof of the eagles' nest. Just as I passed over it, an abominable odour of bones and drying flesh greeted my nostrils. That proved that the eagle—king of birds though he is—is not so clean and tidy as a pigeon. I, for one, prefer a pigeon's nest to an eagle's eyrie.

Soon we reached Gay-Neck and tried to put him in his cage. He was glad to see us, but fought shy of the cage. Since it was getting late, I gave him some lentils to eat. Just about the middle of his meal, seeing him deeply absorbed in eating, I made an effort to grab him with my hand. That frightened the poor bird, and he flew away. The noise of his flight brought the mother eagle out of the inner recess of her nest. She looked out, her beak quivering

and her wings almost opening for flight. At once all
the jungle noises below were stilled, and she sailed
away. We felt that all was over for Gay-Neck. Suddenly a shadow fell upon him. I thought it was the
eagle pouncing; however, it rested on him only a
moment and then receded, but he had had the fright
of his life, and he flew away, driven by sheer terror,
in a zigzag course, far beyond our sight.

I was convinced that we had lost Gay-Neck. But
Ghond insisted that we would find the bird in a day
or two, so we decided to wait and spend our time
there.

Night came on apace, and we sought shelter under some pines. The next morning we were told by
Ghond that the day had come for the young eagles
to fly. He concluded: "Eagles never give their children lessons in flight. They know when their eaglets
are ready for it. Then the parents leave for ever."

All that day the parent eagle did not re-visit her
nest. When night came again her children gave up
all hope of her return, and withdrew into the inner
part of their home. It proved a memorable night
for us. We were so far up that we were quite sure
of no attack by a four-footed beast of prey. Tigers
and leopards go downwards, not that they fear the
heights, but because, like all animals, they follow
their food. Antelopes, deer, water buffalo and wild
boars graze where valleys and jungle-growth are
plentiful, and since they go where grass, sapling, lus-

cious twigs, in short, their dinner, grows on river-banks, those who live by eating them search for them there. That is why, with the exception of birds and a few animals such as wild cats, pythons and snow leopards, the heights are free of beasts of prey. Even the yak, who takes the place of the cow, does not climb so high very frequently or in large numbers. One or two mountain goats one sees occasionally, but nothing larger, and so our night was free of any dramatic experience. But this was amply compensated for by the piercing cold that possessed and shook our bodies in the early dawn. Sleep was out of the question, so I sat up, and wrapping all the blankets of my bedding around me, watched and listened. The stillness was intense—like a drum whose skin had been so stretched that even breathing on it would make it groan. I felt hemmed in by the piercing soundlessness from every direction. Now and then, like an explosion, came the crackling of some dry autumn leaves as a soft-footed wild cat leaped on them from the branch of a tree not far away. That sound very soon sank like a stone in the ever-rising tide of stillness. Slowly, one by one, the stars set. The rising tide of mystery that was reigning everywhere deepened, when like the shaking of lances something shivered in the eagles' eyrie. There was no doubt now that the day was breaking. Again rose the same sound from the same place. The eagles were preening their wings as a man stretches himself before fully waking from sleep. Now I could hear a rustle near by that I thought must be the two eagles coming forward on the front ledge of their nest. Soon came other noises. Storks flew by overhead; strange birds like cranes shouldered the sky. And near by the bellow of a yak tore the stillness asunder as if he had put his horn through the skin of a drum. Far down, birds called one another. At last fell a white light on the Kangchenjunga Range. Then Makalu appeared with an immense halo of opal back of his head. The lower ranges, as high as Mont Blanc, put on their vesture of milk-white glory: shapes and colours of stone and tree leaped into sight. Orchids trembled with morning dew. Now the sun, like a lion, leaped on the shoulder of the sky, and the snow-bastioned horizons bled with scarlet fire.

Ghond and Radja, who were already awake, stood up; then the latter, a well-trained priest, chanted the Sanskrit Vedic prayer to Savitar—the Sun:

> O thou blossom of eastern silence,
> Take thy ancient way untrodden of men.
> Go on thy dustless path of mystery,
> Reach thou the golden throne of God,
>   And be our advocate
> Before His Silence and His compassionate
>   speechlessness.

The prayer frightened the eagles, unaccustomed

to human voices. But ere they were excited to fury, our little ritual was over and we hid ourselves under the stunted pine. The eagles, left without any breakfast, looked out and scanned the sky for a sign of their parent. They gazed below where flocks of parrots and jays flew, as small as humming-birds. Wild geese came trailing across the snowy peaks where they had spent the night on their journey southwards. Soon they too grew as small as beetles, and melted into space. Hour after hour passed, yet no sight of the big eagle! The full-fledged eaglets felt hungrier and hungrier, and began to fret in their nest. We heard a quarrel going on in the interior of the eyrie that grew in intensity and noise till one of them left home in disgust and began to climb the cliff. He went higher and higher. Up and up he walked without using his wings. By now it was past midday; we had luncheon, yet still there was no sight of the parent birds. We judged that the eagle left in the nest was the sister, for she looked smaller than the other eaglet. She sat facing the wind, peering into the distance, but she too grew downhearted. Strange though it may sound, I have yet to see a Himalayan eagle that does not sit facing the wind from the time of its birth until it learns to fly, as a sailor boy might sit looking at the sea until he takes to navigating it. About two in the afternoon, that eagle grew tired of waiting in the nest. She set out in quest of her brother, who was now perching on the top of a cliff far above. He too was facing the wind. As his sister came up, his eyes brightened. He was glad not to be alone, and the sight of her saved him from the melancholy thought of flying for food. No eagle-child have I seen being taught to fly by its parents. That is why younglings will not open their wings until driven by hunger. The parent eagles know this very well, and that is why when their babies grow up, and the time has come, they leave them and go away.

The little sister laboriously climbed till she reached her brother's side, but alas, there was no room for two. Instead of balancing themselves on their perch, the sister's weight knocked her brother almost over. Instantly he opened his wings wide. The wind bore him up. He stretched out his talons, but too late to reach the ground. He was at least two feet up in the air already, so he flapped his wings and rose a little higher. He dipped his tail— which acted like a rudder, and swung him sideways, east, south, east. He swung over us, and we could hear the wind crooning in his wings. Just at that moment a solemn silence fell on everything; the noises of insects stopped; rabbits, if there were rabbits, hid in their holes. Even the leaves seemed to listen in silence to the wing-beats of this new monarch of the air as he sailed higher and higher. And he had to go way up, for only by going very far could he find what he sought. Sometimes eighteen hundred to three thousand feet below him, an eagle sees a hare hopping about on the ground. Then he folds his wings and roars down the air like lightning. The terrible sound of his coming almost hypnotizes the poor creature, and holds him bound to the spot, listening to his enemy's thunderous approach, and then the eagle's talons pierce him.

Seeing her brother go off in this way, and being afraid of loneliness, the sister suddenly spread her wings too. The wind blowing from under threw her up. She also floated in the air and tacked her flight by her tail towards her comrade, and in a few minutes both were lost to sight. Now it was our turn to depart from those hills in search of our pigeon. He might have gone to Dentam. But it behooved us to search every lamasery and baronial castle that had served Gay-Neck as a landmark in his past flights.

On Gay-Neck's Track

AS WE DESCENDED into the bleak oblivion of the gorges below, we suddenly found ourselves in a world of deepening dark, though it was hardly three in the afternoon. It was due to the long shadows of the tall summits under which we moved. We hastened our pace, and the cold air goaded us on. As soon as we had descended about a thousand feet and more, it grew warmer by comparison, but as night came on apace the temperature dropped anew and drove us to seek shelter in a friendly lamasery. We reached that particular *serai* where the lamas, Buddhist monks, most generously offered us hospitality. They spoke to us only as they had occasion in serving us with supper and in escorting us to our rooms. They spend their evenings in meditation.

We had three small cells cut out of the side of a hill, in front of which was a patch of grassy lawn railed off at the outer edges. By the light of the lanthorns we carried, we found that we had only straw mattresses in our stone cells. However, the night passed quickly, for we were so tired that we slept like children in their mothers' arms. About four o'clock next morning I heard many footsteps that roused me completely from sleep. I got out of bed and went in their direction, and soon I discerned bright lights. By climbing down and then up a series of high steps, I reached the central chapel of the lamasery—a vast cave under an overhanging rock, and open on three sides. There before me stood eight lamas with lanthorns that they quietly put away as they then sat down to meditate, their legs crossed under them. The dim light fell on their tawny faces and blue robes, and revealed on their countenances only peace and love.

Presently their leader said to me in Hindustani: "It has been our practise for centuries to pray for all who sleep. At this hour of the night even the insomnia-stricken person finds oblivion; and since men when they sleep cannot possess their conscious thoughts, we pray that Eternal Compassion may purify them, so that when they awake in the morning they will begin their day with thoughts that are pure, kind and brave. Will you meditate with us?"

I agreed readily. We sat praying for compassion for all mankind. Even to this day, when I awake early I think of those Buddhist monks in the Himalayas praying for the cleansing of the thoughts of all men and women still asleep.

The day broke soon enough. I found that we were sitting in a cleft of a mountain, and at our feet lay a precipice sheer and stark. The tinkling of silver bells rose softly in the sunlit air; bells upon bells, silver and golden, chimed gently and filled the air with their sweet music: it was the monks' greeting to the harbinger of light. The sun rose as a clarion cry of triumph—of Light over Darkness, and of Life over Death.

Below, I met Radja and Ghond at breakfast. It was then that a monk who served us said, "Your pigeon came here for shelter yesterday." He gave a description of Gay-Neck, accurate even to the nature of his nose-wattle, its size and colour.

Ghond asked, "How do you know we seek a pigeon?"

The flat-faced lama, without even turning an eyelash, said in a matter-of-fact tone, "I can read your thoughts."

Radja questioned with eagerness: "How can you read our thoughts?"

The monk answered: "If you pray to Eternal Compassion for four hours a day for the happiness of all that live, in the course of a dozen years He gives you the power to read some people's thoughts, especially the thoughts of those who come here. . . . Your pigeon we fed and healed of his fear when he took shelter with us."

"Healed of fear, my Lord!" I exclaimed.

The lama affirmed most simply: "Yes, he was deeply frightened. So I took him in my hands and stroked his head and told him not to be afraid; then yestermorn I let him go. No harm will come to him."

"Can you give your reason for saying so, my Lord?" asked Ghond politely.

The man of God replied to him thus: "You must know, O Jewel amongst hunters, that no animal, nor any man, is attacked and killed by an enemy until the latter succeeds in frightening him. I have seen even rabbits escape hounds and foxes when they kept themselves free of fear. Fear clouds one's wits and paralyses one's nerve. He who allows himself to be frightened lets himself be killed."

"But how do you heal a bird of fear, my Lord?"

To that question of Radja's the holy one answered: "If you are without fear, and you keep not only your thoughts pure but also your sleep untainted of any fear-laden dreams for months, then whatever you touch will become utterly fearless. Your pigeon now is without fear, for I who held him in my hand have not been afraid in thought, deed and dream for nearly twenty years. At present your pet bird is safe: no harm will come to him."

By the calm conviction in his words, spoken without emphasis, I felt that in truth Gay-Neck was safe; and in order to lose no more time, I said farewell to the devotees of Buddha and started south. Let me say that I firmly believe that the lamas were right. If you pray for other people every morning, you can enable them to begin their day with thoughts of purity, courage and love.

Now we dropped rapidly towards Dentam. Our journey lay through places that grew hotter and more familiar. No more did we see the rhododendrons. The autumn that farther up had touched the leaves of trees with crimson, gold, cerise and copper was not so advanced here. The cherry trees still bore their fruits; the moss had grown on trees thickly, and the wind had blown on them the pollen of orchids, large as the palm of your hand, blossoming in purple and scarlet. Many white daturas perspired with dewdrops in the steaming heat of the sun. The trees began to appear taller and more terrible. Bamboos soared upwards like sky-piercing minarets. Creepers as thick as pythons beset our path. The buzzing of the cicada grew insistent and unbearable, and jays jabbered in the woods. Now and then a flock of green parrots flung their emerald glory in the face of the sun, then vanished. Insects multiplied. Mammoth butterflies, velvety black, swarmed from blossom to blossom, and innumerable small birds preyed on numberless buzzing flies.

We were stung with the sharpest stings of worms, and now and then we had to wait to let pass a serpent that crossed our path. Were it not for the practised eyes of Ghond, who knew which way the animals came and went, we would have been killed ten times over by a snake or a buffalo. Sometimes Ghond would put his ear to the ground, and listen. After several minutes he would say: "Ahead of us, buffalos are coming. Let us wait till they pass." And soon enough we would hear their sharp hoofs moving through the undergrowth with a sinister noise as if a vast scythe were cutting, cutting, cutting the very ground from under our feet. Yet we pressed on, stopping for half an hour for lunch. At last we reached the borders of Sikkim, whose small valley glimmered with ripening red millet, green oranges and golden bananas, set against hillsides glittering with marigolds above which softly shone the violets.

Just then we came to a sight that I shall never forget. At our feet on the narrow caravan road the air burned in iridescence: the heat was so great that it vibrated with colours. Hardly had we gone a few yards when like a thunderclap rose a vast flock of Himalayan pheasants; then they flew into the jungle, their wings burning like peacocks' plumes in the warm air. We kept on moving. In another couple of minutes flew up another flock but these were mud-coloured birds. In my perplexity I asked Ghond for an explanation.

He said: "Do you not see, O Beloved of Felicity,

the caravan that passed here was loaded with millet? One of their sacks had a hole in it. A few handfuls of millet leaked out on the road before the sack was sewn up. Later on arrived these birds, and fed themselves here. We came upon them suddenly and frightened them to flight."

"But, O Diadem of Wisdom," I asked, "why do the males look so gorgeous and why are the females mud-coloured? Is nature always partial to the male?"

Ghond made the following explanation: "It is said that Mother Nature has given all birds the colours that hide them from their enemies. But do you not see that those pheasants are so full of splendour that they can be sighted and killed even by a blind man?"

Radja exclaimed, "Can they?"

Ghond answered: "O, wary beyond thy years, no! The real reason is that they live on trees, and do not come down before the earth is very hot. In this hot India of ours the air two inches above the ground is so burning that it quivers with a thousand colours; and the plumage of the pheasant is similar. When we look at them we do not see birds, but the many-coloured air that camouflages them completely. We almost walked on them a few moments ago, thinking them but a part of the road at our feet."

"That I comprehend," resumed Radja reverently. "But why did the female look mud-coloured and why did they not fly away with the male?"

Ghond answered without hesitation: "When the enemy approaches and takes them by surprise, the male flies up to face the enemy's bullets, though without thought of chivalry. The females' wings are not so good. Besides, she, being of the colour of the earth, opens her wings to shelter her babies under them, then lies flat on the ground, completely melting away her identity into that colour scheme. After the enemy goes away in quest of the corpses of their already slaughtered husbands, the females run away with their babies into the nearest thicket. . . . And if it is not too late in the year, and if their grown-up babies are not with them, the mother birds singly flop to the ground and lie there, making the gesture of protecting their young. Self-sacrifice becomes a habit with them, and habitually they put forth their wings whether they have any young ones with them or not. That is what they were doing when we came upon them; then suddenly they realized that they were without anyone to protect, and as we still kept on coming down upon them they took to flight, poor fliers though they are."

With the approach of dusk we took shelter in the house of a Sikkimese nobleman whose son was a friend of ours. There we found further traces of Gay-Neck, who had been to their house many times before, and so when he reached the familiar place on his latest visit he had eaten millet seeds, drunk water and taken his bath. Also, he had preened his wings and left two small azure feathers that my friend had preserved for the sake of their colouring. When I saw them my heart leaped in joy, and that night I slept in utter peace and contentment. There was another reason for sleeping well, for Ghond had told us to rest deeply, as after the following day's march we were to spend the night in the jungle.

The next night, when we sat on that tree-top in the deep jungle, often did I think of the home of my Sikkimese friend and its comforts.

Imagine yourself marching all day, then spending the night on a vast banyan tree in the very heart of a dangerous forest! It took us a little over half an hour to find that tree, for banyans do not often grow in high altitudes, and also the same reason that made us choose the banyan made us look for a very large one of its kind—it would be of no use to us if it were slender enough for an elephant to break down by walking backwards against it! That is how the pachyderm destroys some very stout trees. We looked for something tall, and so stout that no elephant could reach its upper branches with his trunk and not even two tuskers could break it by pushing against it with their double weight.

At last we found a tree to our liking. Radja stood on Ghond's shoulder, and I on Radja's, until we reached branches as thick as a man's torso. I climbed and sat on one of them and from it let down our rope ladder that we always carried in the jungle for emergencies such as the present one. Radja climbed up and sat near me; then Ghond ascended the branch and sat between us. Now we saw that below us where Ghond had stood it had not only grown dark as the heart of a coal-mine, but there glowed two green lights set very close to each other. We knew too well whose they were. Ghond exclaimed jovially, "Had I been delayed down there two extra minutes, the striped fellow would have killed me."

Seeing that his prey had escaped him, the tiger gave a thunderous yell, scourging the air like a curse. At once a tense silence fell, and smothered all the noises of insects and little beasts, and it descended further and deeper until it sank into the earth and seemed to grip the very roots of the trees.

We made ourselves secure on our perch, and Ghond passed the extremely flexible rope ladder around his waist, then Radja's, then mine, fastening the rest of it around the main trunk of the tree. We tested it by letting it bear the weight of one of us at a time. This precaution was taken for the purpose of preventing a sleep-stricken member of our group from slipping down to the floor of the jungle, for after all, in sleep the body relaxes so that it falls like a stone. Finally, Ghond arranged his arms for pillows for our heads when slumber came.

Now that we had taken all the necessary precautions, we concentrated our attention on what was happening below. The tiger had vanished from under our tree. The insects had resumed their song, which was again and again stilled for a few seconds as huge shapes fell from far-off trees with soft thuds. Those were leopards and panthers who had slept on the trees all day and were now leaping down to hunt at night.

When they had gone the frogs croaked, insects buzzed continually and owls hooted. Noise, like a diamond, opened its million facets. Sounds leaped at one's hearing like the dart of sunlight into unprotected eyes. A boar passed, cracking and breaking all before him. Soon the frogs stopped croaking, and way down on the floor of the jungle we heard the tall grass and other undergrowth rise like a haycock, then with a sigh fall back. That soft sinister sigh like the curling up of spindrift drew nearer and nearer, then . . . it slowly passed our tree. Oh, what a relief! It was a constrictor going to the water-hole. We stayed on our tree-top as still as its bark—Ghond was afraid that our breathing might betray our position to the terrible python.

A few minutes later we heard one or two snappings of small twigs almost as faint as a man cracking his fingers. It was a stag whose antlers had got caught in some vines, and he was snapping them to get himself freed. Hardly had he passed when the jungle grew very tense with expectation. Sounds began to die down. Out of the ten or a dozen different noises that we had heard all at once, there now re-

With enormously long reach he almost touched the top of the tree.   page 68

mained only three: the insects' tick tack tock, the short wail of the stag—no doubt the constrictor was strangling him near the water-hole—and the wind overhead. Now the elephants were coming. Hatis (elephants), about fifty in a herd, came and played around the place below us. The squeal of the females, the grunt of the males, and the run run run of the babies filled the air.

I do not remember what happened next, for I had dozed off into a sort of waking sleep, and in that condition I heard myself talking pigeon-language to Gay-Neck. I was experiencing a deep confusion of sleep and dream. Someone shook and roused me. To my utter amazement Ghond whispered: "I cannot hold you any more. Wake up! Mischief is abroad. A mad elephant has been left behind. The straggler is bent on harm. We are not high enough to be altogether out of the reach of his trunk, and if he raises it far enough he will scent our presence. Wild elephants hate and fear man, and once he gets our odour he may stay about here all day in order to find out where we are. Rouse thy vigilance, lad. Draw the blade of alertness before the enemy strikes."

There was no mistake about that elephant. In the pale light of early dawn I could discern a sort of hillock darkly moving about under our tree. He was going from tree to tree and snapping off a few succulent twigs that autumn had not yet blighted. He seemed greedy and bent on gorging himself with those delicacies, rare for the time of the year. In about half an hour he performed a strange trick, putting his fore-feet on the bole of a thick tree, and swinging up his trunk. It gave him the appearance of a far-spreading mammoth; with that enormously long reach he almost touched the top of the tree, and twisted the most delectable branches off its boughs. After having denuded it of its good twigs, he came to a tree next to ours, and there did the same thing. Now he found a slender tree that he pulled down with his trunk, and placed his fore-feet on the poor bent thing and broke it with a crash under his own weight. He ate all that he could of that one. While he was breakfasting thus, his rampage frightened the birds and monkeys, who flew in the air or ran from tree to tree jabbering in terror. Then the elephant put his feet on the stump of the broken tree and reached up into ours until he touched the branch on which we sat. Hardly had he done so when he squealed, for the odour of man all beasts fear, and swiftly withdrew his trunk. After grunting and complaining to himself, he put up his trunk again very near Ghond's face. Just then Ghond sneezed almost into the elephant's nostrils. That struck panic into the latter's heart; he felt beleaguered by men. Trumpeting and squealing like a frightened fiend, he dashed through the jungle, breaking and smashing everything before him.

Again the parrots, thick as green sails, flew in the sky. Monkeys screamed and raced from tree to tree. Boars and stags stampeded on the floors of the jungle. For a while the din and tumult reigned unchecked. We had to wait some time before we dared to descend from our perch in order to resume our homeward journey.

Late that day we reached home after being carried on horseback by a caravan that we were fortunate enough to meet. All three of us were dead tired, but we forgot our fatigue when we beheld Gay-Neck in his nest in our house at Dentam. Oh, what joy! That evening, before I went to sleep, I thought of the calm, quiet assurance of the lama who said, "Your bird is safe."

Gay-Neck's Truancy

BUT THE DAY AFTER our return Gay-Neck flew away again, in the morning, and failed to put in an appearance later. We waited for him most anxiously during four successive days, and then, unable to bear the suspense any longer, Ghond and I set out in search of him, determined to find him, dead or alive. This time we hired two ponies to take us as far as Sikkim. We had made sure of our path by asking people about Gay-Neck in each village that we had to pass through. Most of them had seen the bird, and some of them gave an accurate description of him: one hunter had seen him in a lamasery nesting next to a swift under the eaves of the house; another, a Buddhist monk,

said that he had seen him near their monastery in
Sikkim on a river-bank where wild ducks had their
nest, and in the latest village that we passed through
on the second afternoon we were told that he was
seen in the company of a flock of swifts.

Led by such good accounts we reached the highest table-land of Sikkim and were forced to bivouac
there the third night. Our ponies were sleepy, and
so were we, but after what seemed like an hour's
sleep, I was roused by a tenseness that had fallen
upon everything. I found the two beasts of burden
standing stiff; in the light of the fire and that of the
risen half-moon I saw that their ears were raised
tensely in the act of listening carefully. Even their
tails did not move. I too listened intently. There was
no doubt that the silence of the night was more than
mere stillness; stillness is empty, but the silence that
beset us was full of meaning, as if a God, shod with
moonlight, was walking so close that if I were to
put out my hand I could touch his garment.

Just then the horses moved their ears as if to
catch the echo of a sound that had moved imper-
ceptibly through the silence. The great deity had
gone already; now a queer sensation of easing the
tense atmosphere set in. One could feel even the
faintest shiver of the grass, but that too was momentary; the ponies now listened for a new sound
from the north. They were straining every nerve in
the effort. At last even I could hear it. Something

like a child yawning in his sleep became audible. Stillness again followed. Then a sighing sound, long drawn out, ran through the air, and sank lower and lower, like a thick green leaf slowly sinking through calm water. Then rose a murmur on the horizon as if someone were praying against the sky-line. About a minute later the horses relaxed their ears and switched their tails, and I, too, felt myself at ease. Lo! thousands of geese were flying through the upper air. They were at least four thousand feet above us, but all the same the ponies had heard their coming long before I did.

The flight of the geese told us that dawn was at hand, and I sat up and watched. The stars set one by one. The ponies began to graze. I gave them more rope; now that the night had passed, they did not need to be tied so close to the fire.

In another ten minutes the intense stillness of the dawn held all things in its grip, and that had its effect on our two beasts. This time I could clearly see both of them lifting their heads and listening. What sounds were they trying to catch? I did not have long to wait. In a tree not far off a bird shook itself; then another did the same thing, on another bough. One of them sang. It was a song-sparrow, and its cry roused all nature. Other song-sparrows trilled; then other birds, and still others! By now shapes and colours were coming to light with blinding rapidity. Thus passed the short tropical twilight, and Ghond got up to say his prayers.

That day our wanderings brought us to the lamasery near Singalila of which I have spoken before. The lamas were glad to give us all the news of Gay-Neck. They informed me that the previous afternoon Gay-Neck and the flock of swifts who nested under the eaves of the monastery had flown southwards.

Again with the blessings of the lamas we said farewell to their hospitable *serai,* and set out on Gay-Neck's trail. The mountains burned like torches behind us as we bestowed on them our last look. Before us lay the autumn-tinted woods glimmering in gold, purple, green and cerise.

Gay-Neck's Story

IN THE PRECEDING chapter I made scanty references to the places and incidents through which Gay-Neck was recovered. Ghond found his track with certainty the first day of our ten days' search for him, but in order to see those things clearly and continuously, it would be better to let Gay-Neck tell his own Odyssey. It is not hard for us to understand him if we use the grammar of fancy and the dictionary of imagination.

The October noon when we boarded the train at Darjeeling for our return journey to town, Gay-Neck sat in his cage, and commenced the story of his recent truancy from Dentam to Singalila and back.

"O master of many tongues, O wizard of all languages human and animal, listen to my tale. Listen to the stammering, wandering narrative of a poor bird. Since the river has its roots in the hill, so springs my story from the mountains.

"When near the eagles' nest I heard and beheld the wicked hawk's talons tear my mother to pieces, I was so distressed that I decided to die, but not by the claws of those treacherous birds. If I was to be served up for a meal, let it be to the king of the air; so I went and sat on the ledge near the eagles' nest, but they would do me no harm. Their house was in mourning. Their father had been trapped and killed, and their mother was away hunting for pheasants and hares. Since up to now the younglings had eaten only what had been killed for them, they dared not attack and finish poor me who was alive. I do not know yet why no eagle has harmed me; during the past days I have seen many.

"Then you came to catch and cage me. As I was in no mood for human company, I flew away, taking my chances as I went, but I remembered places and persons who were your friends and I stayed with them on my way south to Dentam. During those two days—for I flew only two days—I was attacked by a newly fledged hawk, and I gave him the best defeat of his life. It was in this wise; one morning as I was flying over the woods below Sikkim, I heard the wind screech overhead. I knew what that meant now, so I played a trick. I stopped all on a sudden, and the hawk, who was falling upon me, missed me and fell way down, grazing his wing on a tree-top. I rose higher and flew fast, but he caught up, and then I began to make circles in the air. I rose high, oh, so high that my lungs could not breathe the air there, and I had to come down again.

"But no sooner had I descended than with an ominous screech and cry the hawk fell upon me. Fortunately, then and there, for the first time in my life I tried to tumble as I had seen my father do, and I succeeded in making a double tumble, then shooting up like a fountain. Again the hawk missed and rose to attack, but I gave him no chance. I flew at him. And just as I was passing him, he dipped down, then up, and clutched at me; again I tumbled, striking him so hard that he lost his balance. I do not know what happened, but that very moment I felt something sucking me down, down to the depth of the earth. My wings were powerless. I fell as an eagle falls—heavy and inevitable—striking the hawk on the head with my full weight. I think the blow stunned him. He too fell, and was lost in the woods below, but I was glad to find myself on the branch of an ilex tree.

"I had been sucked down by an air current. Since that first experience of mine, I have met many others like it, but I have never understood why it was that above certain trees and streams the air gets very cold and makes a current that draws into itself the bird that strikes it. I had to learn the lesson of flying in those currents after being whirled up and down by them. But I do not hate them, since the first air current I encountered saved my life.

"Sitting on that ilex tree, I became so hungry that it drove me to fly home. Luckily, no soulless hawk obstructed my arrow-like flight.

"But my successful escape from that newly fledged murderer gave me back my courage, and as soon as you came home I said to myself: 'Now that he, my friend, has seen me alive, he will not worry about me. I must fly anew through the falcon-infested air and test my courage.'

"Now began my real Odyssey. I went northwards to the eagles' nest, and stopped at the lamasery where a holy man had blessed me on an earlier occasion. There I re-visited Mr. and Mrs. Swift, my old friends. Moving farther north, I went past Singalila at last and reached the eyrie of the eagles who had flown away. So I made myself comfortable there, but not too happy, for the eagles leave all kinds of refuse in their nests, and I am afraid they swarm with vermin. Though I spent my day in the eagles' nest, I decided to spend the night in a tree, free from horrid insects. After a couple of days, my going in and out of the eyrie gave me great prestige among other birds. They feared me, perhaps because they took me for a sort of eagle. Even the hawks began to give me a wide berth. That gave me all the confidence that I needed, so early one morning, seeing a white wedge of birds coming south, flying very high, I joined them. They did not mind my joining them; they were wild geese going towards Ceylon and beyond, in the quest of a sunny ocean.

"Those geese, after two hours' flight, as the day became warmer, descended onto a rapid mountain stream. Unlike the eagles, they rarely looked downwards, but watched the horizon lines. They spied a little ribbon of whitish-blue far off against the sky, and flew in a slowly declining straight line till it seemed as if the earth were rising to meet us, and soon all plunged into the silver stream, for now the waters looked more silvery than blue. They floated on the water, but as I knew that I was not web-footed, I sat on a tree and watched their antics. You know how flat and ugly the bills of geese are, but now I saw the reason for it. They used them like pincers on things such as shells that grew on the side of the banks. Every now and then a goose would put his bill on a plant or a shell, then wring it out of position as a butcher would wring a duck's neck. After that it would devour its victim wholesale, crushing it in its powerful throat, but ere it passed very far down its size dwindled to nothing. I saw one fellow do worse than that. He found a fish —as lean as a water-snake—in a hole under the bank; he began to pull it. The more he pulled, the thinner and longer it got. Slowly, after a terrific tug of war, the poor fellow was dragged from his hole.

Then the goose hopped up the shore and flung it on the ground. His bill had crushed the part it had held onto, nearly into pulp, so no wonder his wriggling victim was already dead. Then from nowhere walked up to him another goose. (By the way, are not geese the most ungainly birds when they are not flying or swimming? On the water they resemble dreams floating on pools of sleep, but on land they hobble like cripples on crutches!) By now the two geese were quarrelling. They pulled each other's feathers; they slapped with their wings; they kicked each other with their feet every time they hopped up above the ground. While they were thus engaged, oblivious of their bone of contention, a cat-like creature, probably an otter, pounced from among the reeds, grabbed the dead eel, and vanished. Now the geese declared a truce, but too late! Oh, they have no more sense than, well—geese! Compared with them, we pigeons seem paragons of cleverness.

"After they had stopped fighting, the chief goose cried—'Cluck, caw, caw, caw!' That instant all of them paddled hard to gather momentum. A few extra wing-beats and they were in the air. How beautiful they looked now! That soft soughing of vast wings, their necks and bodies like drawings against the sky, making a severe eye-pleasing wedge. I shall never forget it.

"But every flock has its straggler. One fellow was left behind, because he was still struggling with a fish. At last he secured it, and flew up in quest of a tree where he could eat it under cover. Suddenly from the empty air an enormous hawk attacked him. The goose rose higher, but the indefatigable hawk did not relent. Up and up they circled, screaming and quacking. Suddenly a faint but clear echo of a honk was heard. The chief of the flock was calling the straggler; that distracted him. Hardly knowing what he was doing, he honked back an answer. That instant the fish fell from his mouth. It began to fall like a leaf. The hawk dipped, and just as he was going to pierce it with his talons, down the air came a surge and roar. In a trice an eagle fell as a rock falls down a high precipice. That hawk ran for his life, and that gave me a great deal of pleasure to behold.

"Under the eagle's two wings like vast sails, the talons forked out lightning fashion and grabbed the fish—then the monarch of the air in his shining armour of brown gold sailed away, the wind ruffling the feathers above his knees. Far away, the hawk was still running for his life!

"I am glad he went very far away, for I had to fly about in quest of a caravan road where I could get some seeds dropped by men. I soon found some, and after a tolerably decent meal I perched on a tree and went to sleep. When I woke it was mid-afternoon. I decided to fly way up, to reach the blessed lamasery, and visit my friends the swifts. My flight was unattended by any mishap, for I had learned to fly carefully by now. I generally went very far up and looked down, as well as at the horizon. Though I have not so long a neck as a wild goose, yet I turned and took side glances every few minutes in order to make sure that nothing was attacking my rear.

"I reached the monastery just in time, as the lamas were getting ready to stand on the edge of their chapel in order to pour benediction upon the world during sunset. Mr. and Mrs. Swift were flying near the nest where their three youngsters were put to bed. Of course, they were glad to receive me. After their vesper services, the monks fed me, and the sweet old lama said something about a blessing that someone called Infinite Compassion had put upon me. Then I flew from his hand feeling absolutely fearless. In that state of mind and body I entered my nest next to the swifts under the eaves of the lamasery.

"The nights in October are cold. In the morning, while the priests rang their bells, the little swifts flew about for exercise while their parents and I had to fly to shake off the chill of the morning. That day I spent there in order to help them make preparations for their journey south. I was surprised to learn that they intended to build a nest in Ceylon or Africa whither they were going. They explained to me that a swift's nest is not at all any easy thing to construct. Then in order to assuage my thirst for knowledge, they told me how they erect their homes."

Gay-Neck's Odyssey *(continued)*

"IN ORDER TO MAKE clear to you the swift's skill at architecture, let me first of all draw attention to the swift's handicaps. He has a small beak fit for catching flying insects. His mouth is very wide to enable him to catch his prey while he is on the wing. Very few insects can escape his wide-open mouth as he comes down on them. As he is very small, Mr. Swift cannot lift much weight. No wonder his house is built out of slender materials such as straw and twigs of trees no thicker than a middle-sized needle.

"The first time I saw a swift he looked paralysed and deformed. All swifts know that they have wretched legs. The bird has hardly any legs to balance upon. His small feet like fish-hooks, made for sticking on to places, emerge right out of his body; his little hooklike claws seem inflexible. He has not enough leg between his body and his feet, and this deprives him of the springiness that longer legs supply to other birds. No wonder he cannot hop or jump. But that defect is squared by his one advantage—he can cling to stone palisades, marble eaves, and alabaster friezes of houses as no other bird can. I have seen my friend Swift hang on to polished walls as if they were corrugated surfaces.

"Under these handicaps, all he can do is to choose holes in walls just under the eaves for his home. But there he cannot lay his eggs, for they would roll off. So he catches flying straws and small falling leaves, and glues them to the stone floor of his nest with his saliva. That is the secret of his skill at architecture. His saliva is wonderful; it dries and hardens like the best glue of the cabinet-makers. When the nest is made ready, the long white eggs are laid. Among the swifts, women are not so emancipated as among the pigeons. Our women enjoy equal rights with men, but the female swift has always the larger part of the work to do. For instance, Mr. Swift never sits on the eggs; he lets his wife do it. Occasionally he brings her food during the day, but otherwise he spends all his waking hours visiting male swifts whose wives are similarly occupied. I told my friend Swift he ought to copy the pigeons and give more freedom to his wife, but he seemed to think this a pet joke of mine.

"At last our preparations were made, and one fine autumn morning the five swifts and I set out in a southerly direction, piloted by Mr. Swift. We never went in a straight line, but zigzagged east or west, though we held to a general southern course. The swifts eat flies and gnats that float on rivers and lakes. They go about fifty miles an hour—a blinding speed for a small bird—and do not like woods because while their gaze is fixed downwards in search of insects, they may break their wings on a tree. They prefer open clear spaces above the waters, and with their scythelike long wings they cleave the air as swiftly as an eagle falls on its prey. Think of the precision of the swift's eye and mouth! While he is whirling over the water, he snaps up flying insects with such ease that the space he traverses is completely cleared of all the gnats and flies who a few moments before danced in the sunlight.

"Thus we went over streams, ponds and lagoons. By the way, Mr. Swift eats his food in a hurry and takes his drink the same way. He flies over the water, skimming up drops as he goes, and swallowing them at a very high rate of speed. No wonder that he hates to fly in a place crowded with boughs, larches and saplings.

"But so much flight in open air has its drawbacks. While a swift is eating insects with such speed, a sparrow-hawk may fall on him from above. Under these circumstances the swift cannot dip down, for that would mean death by drowning. I must tell you of one such attack on my friends. They were busy catching their dinner on a vast lake one afternoon, and while I was flying about, keeping an eye on the younger swifts, down came a sparrow-hawk. I who had undertaken to look after the children had to act quickly even at the risk of my own life. Without an instant's hesitation I plunged and tumbled, inserting my body between the enemy and the young ones. Well, the sparrow-hawk had never expected so much nerve from a member of the dove family, nor did he calculate my weight. I was at least five ounces heavier than he. He struck my tail with his talons, tore a few feathers, and thinking that he had got something he circled the air for a moment or two. Before he realized that he had only my feathers, all the swifts were safe, clinging to the bark of a tree out of anybody's reach. But the small sparrow-hawk was so infuriated that he fell on me with the fury of a large one. However, his body was very small and his talons smaller, and I knew they could not pierce my feathers and my skin very far. So I accepted his challenge and tumbled up. He followed. I shot downwards; he too dived after. Then I began to rise high. He pursued as before. But those little hawks fear the upper air, and his wings lagged now. To my two wing-beats he could make but one. Seeing him hopeless and tired, I planned to teach him the lesson of his life. No sooner had I conceived than I executed my plan. I shot downwards. He plunged after. Down, down, down! The water of the lake rose towards us, higher and higher every second till it looked no farther than the width of my wing. Then I flung forward a few inches and struck a warm air current that helped me upwards. As you know, air warmed in the hollow places and valleys of mountain country has a tendency to shoot up into cooler regions. We birds look for these currents to help us when we have need to make a sudden upward flight. Now I tumbled three times, and when I looked down I found that sparrow-hawk drowning in the water. He had not been able to reach the air current. After a considerable ducking, he laboriously flew ashore, and there under thick leaves hid his disgrace. That instant the swifts came out of their hiding-place and flew southwards.

"The next day we met some wild ducks. They had coloured throats like mine, but otherwise they were as white as snow. They were stream ducks, whose habit is to float down a mountain brook after fish. When they have gone far, they rise out of the water and fly back to their starting-place. So they spend the day like shuttles going back and forth. Their bills were flatter than those of the geese, and they are dented inside, for once they close on a fish the bills never slip. They did not seem to care much for the shellfish, but that was probably because the fish in the lake were so plentiful. The swifts did not like the place because the ducks' wings beat the air continually and blew away the insects that normally fly over any water surface. Still, they were glad to see ducks that loved and lived on mountain torrents, never bothering about the calm water so dear to most ducks.

"It was these ducks who warned us against the owls and other murderers of the night that infested those regions. So we did our best to hide in places too small for owls to go into. It was easy to find holes in a tree small enough for the swifts, but I decided to stay in the open and take my chances. Night came on apace. Pretty soon my eyes could serve me no longer. Darkness within darkness, like layers of black cloth, lay upon them. I commended myself to the Gods of my race and tried to sleep. But who could sleep with those owls who-whoing about? Terror seized me for the night. Not an hour passed without some bird's shrieking in pain. The owls, too, hooted in triumph. Now a starling, then a bulbul (the Indian nightingale) would cry mortally, and die under the owl's grip. Though my eyes were shut, my ears knew the carnage that went on. A crow shrieked. Then another, then another. Almost a flock flew up in terror and smashed themselves against trees. But better that kind of death than to be killed by the searing and tearing beaks and claws of the owls. Soon to my utter confusion I smelt weasels in the air, and then I felt that death was at hand. That made me desperate; I opened my eyes to see. A pale while light was shining on all things. There before me, about six feet away, was a weasel. I flew up, though that increased the danger of my being killed by the owls. And sure enough, along came one, hooting and screaming. Two more owls followed. I heard their wing-beats, and by the nature of the sounds I knew that we were flying over the water, for it echoed back even the slightest shiver of our feathers. I could not fly in any direction very far, since I saw not more than six feet at a time, so I waited in the air, groping for a current that sucked the air of the river up above the boughs that hung over it. Alas, those owls were on me already, but I tumbled, then swung into a circle. The owls would not give up the chase. I rose farther up. Now the moonlight like water dripped from my wings. I could see a little more clearly, and that brought me back my courage. But my enemies did not relent. They too rose, and more light fell on their eyes, blinding them, though not completely. Suddenly two of them plunged towards me. Up I flew. The owls missed—lo! they had fallen on each other. Their claws locked together, their wings flapping helplessly in the air, they screamed like fiends and fell among the reeds of the river-bank.

"Now I looked about carefully and noticed to my

surprise that I had flown towards the dawning of day and not at the moon. My terror-stricken eyes had not seen truly. But there were no more owls about; they had begun to seek for places of hiding from the growing sunlight. Although I felt safe, I kept away from the prodigious shadows of the tall trees, for even now an owl might lurk there. I stayed on a slender branch on a tree-top that caught the first flight of the sun's arrows, transfiguring it into an umbrella of dancing gold. Slowly the light spread farther down till the white torrent below trembled with colours like a weasel's eyes.

"Just then on the river-bank I saw an appalling sight. Two large crows, blacker than coal, were jabbing and prodding with their beaks a helpless blinking owl, caught in the reeds. Now that ·the sun shone, it could not open its eyes. Of course the night's slaughter done among the crows was large, and it was the crows' turn to avenge their wrongs, but I could not bear the sight of two of them killing that trapped owl. So I flew away from the murderers and went to seek my friends the swifts. I recounted some of my experiences, and the parents told me that they had heard terrible cries of distress that kept them from slumber. Mr. Swift asked if everything was safe outside, and I thought it was. When we came out, I found that poor owl lying dead, among the reeds!

"Strange to say, that morning we saw no ducks on

the stream. Apparently they had flown very early in the morning in a southerly direction, and we decided to do the same. We planned not to seek the company of other birds going our way. For during the season of migration, wherever flocks of pigeons, grouse and other birds go, their enemies, such as owls, hawks and eagles, go after them. In order to avoid danger and such shocking sights as we had seen before, we flew to the east, and after going eastwards a whole day, we rested in the village of Sikkim. The next day we flew south for half a day, and again eastwards. That sort of roundabout journey took a long time, but it saved us no end of trouble. Once we were overtaken by a storm, and were blown into a lake country, and there I saw an amazing sight. I was on a tree-top, when below me I discerned a lot of domesticated ducks floating on the water, each one with a fish in its mouth. But none of them swallowed his morsel. I had never seen ducks resist the temptation to eat fish before, so I called the swifts to behold the sight. They clung to the barks of several trees and looked at the ducks, but they could hardly believe their eyes. What was the matter with them? Pretty soon a boat heaved in sight, poled by two men, flat-faced and yellow. On seeing them, the ducks paddled to the boat as fast as they could go. Reaching it, they hopped up, and then—can you believe it?—they dropped their capture into a large fish basket, and jumped down into the lake to fish for some more, and that went on for at least two hours. Apparently those Tibeto-Burman fishermen never cast nets. They tied a string tightly, almost to the choking point, around their ducks' necks, and then brought them to the lake to catch fish. Whatever the latter caught, they brought to their human masters. However, when their basket became full, they undid the strings that were around the ducks' necks, who then plunged into the lake, and gorged themselves on fish.

"Now we flew away far from the lakes for a while in quest of harvest-fields. There the swifts fell on the insects that flew about newly mown grain, and devoured them. I, too, ate to repletion of the grain, though not of the insects. While sitting on the fence of a rice-field, I heard someone hitting something. It sounded very much like a chaffinch cracking open a cherry-stone with his beak in order to get at its kernel. (Isn't it strange that a little bird's beak has the power of a nutcracker?) But, when I wandered nearer the place, under the fence, whence the noise was coming, I found another bird—a Himalayan thrush. He was engaged, not in cracking cherry-stones, but in hitting a slowly moving snail with his beak. Tick, tack; tick, tack—tack! He hammered on and on until the snail was stunned into stillness. The thrush raised his head and looked around, poised himself on tiptoe, opened his wings, took a quick aim and struck three more blows—tack, tack,

tack! The shell broke open, revealing a delicious snail. He lifted it up with his beak, which was bleeding slightly; apparently he had opened his mouth too wide and hurt its corners. After balancing the snail correctly in his grasp, he flew up and vanished into a tree where his mate was waiting for supper.

"The rest of our journey through the grain fields of Sikkim was uneventful. The only thing that is worth remembering was the trapping of peacocks by men in the forests. These birds come to the hot southern marshes in quest of food and warmth when the snakes and other creatures whom they eat go into winter quarters in the north.

"Peacocks and tigers admire one another. The former like to look at the tiger's skin, and he enjoys the beauty of their plumes. Sometimes at the water-hole a tiger will stand gazing at the plumes of a peacock on a bough, and the peacock will crane his neck to feast his eyes on the beauty of the striped skin. Now comes man, the eternal aggressor, on the scene. For instance, a man one day brought a piece of cloth painted exactly like a tiger's skin, so that no bird could tell by looking at it that it was not the striped one himself. Then he set a noose on a branch of a tree nearby, and slunk away. I could tell by the odour of the painted cloth that it was not a tiger, but peacocks have no sense of smell worth speaking of. They are victims of their own eyes. So in a few hours a pair of peacocks came and began to gaze at the make-believe tiger from a tree-top, coming lower and lower. They deceived themselves into the belief that the tiger was asleep. Emboldened by that illusion, they came very close and stood on the branch near the trap. It did not take them long to walk into it, but how they both stepped into a single trap I cannot make out. No sooner were they caught than they shrieked in despair. Then appeared the trapper, and played another trick on them. He threw up two large black canvas caps and lassoed them on each peacock's head, hiding the poor bird's eyes. Once the eyes are darkened, a bird never resists much. The man now tied their feet so that they could not walk; then he set one on each end of his bamboo pole. Slowly he lifted it by the middle, put it on his shoulder and walked off, the long tails of the peacocks streaming down like cataracts of rainbow before and behind him.

"There ends my Odyssey. The next day I said good-bye to the swifts. They went farther south, and I was glad to get home, a wiser and a sadder bird. Now," demanded Gay-Neck, "tell me this: Why is there so much killing and inflicting of pain by birds and beasts on one another? I don't think all of you men hurt each other. Do you? But birds and beasts do. All that makes me so sad."

PART TWO

Gay-Neck's Training
for War

AFTER WE RE-turned to town, the air was filled with the rumours of a coming war somewhere in Europe. Now that winter was at hand, I decided to give Gay-Neck such training as would be necessary in case he was asked to be a carrier for the British War Department. Since he was used to the climate of the northeastern Himalayas, he would be an invaluable messenger for the army in any European country. Even now, with the aid of wireless telegraph and radio, no army can dispense with the help of carrier-pigeons. All that will become clear to you as the present story unfolds itself.

In training carriers for war work, I followed a

plan of my own that Ghond approved. By the way, the old fellow came all the way to town with us. He stayed in our house two or three days, then decided to leave, saying: "The city is unbearable. I never loved any city, but this one frightens me with its electric tramway and *how-aghari* [wind chariot] —the automobile. If I do not shake the dust of this town off my feet very soon, I shall be nothing better than a coward. A tiger in the jungle does not frighten me, but I cannot say the same of an automobile. One crossing of a modern city street imperils more lives in a minute than a day in the most dangerous forests. Farewell! I go where the woods wear stillness for a dress, the air is free of odours and dust, and the sky, a hollowed turquoise, is not cross-cut and pierced with poles and telegraph wires. Instead of factory whistles I shall hear the song of birds; and in the place of thieves and gunmen I shall have innocent tigers and panthers face to face. Farewell!"

But before he left, he helped me to buy about forty more carriers, and some tumblers. You may ask me the reason of my preference for these two kinds. I do not know that I have any exclusive love for tumblers and carriers, but it is true that fan-tails, pouters and other pigeons are more ornamental than useful. In our house we had some of these varieties, but they proved so difficult to keep in company with the carriers and travellers that I finally bestowed all my appreciation on pure flyers.

In India we have a queer custom that I do not like. If you sell a carrier, no matter at what fabulous price, and it flies away from its new owner and comes back to you, it becomes your property again, and no matter what the value, you never refund the price. Knowing that to be the accepted custom among pigeon-fanciers, I had to train my newly acquired pets before anything else to love me. Since I had paid for them, I did not wish them to return to their former owners. I did my very best to make them cherish their new home loyally. But life is practical. I had to begin with the most necessary steps. The first few weeks I had to tie up their wings in order to keep them completely within the bounds of our roof. The art of tying a pigeon's feathers so that he is prevented from flying is delicate. You take a thread, and pass one end of it over one feather and under the next, very near its root, all the way until the entire wing is encompassed. Then you pass the other end of the thread by the same process under the first, over the second, and so on to the end of the wing, where the two ends of the thread are tied. It is very much like darning. It is an utterly painless form of captivity, for though it prevents a pigeon from flying, yet he is not kept from opening or flapping his wings. He can stretch them and can massage them with his beak. After this, I used to put my new pigeons at different corners of the roof so that they might sit still, and with their eyes take in the colour and quality of their new surroundings.

At least fifteen days should be allowed for this process.

Here I must record a cunning thing that Gay-Neck did when his wings were tied in the above manner. I sold him early in November just to see if he would return to me when his wings were freed from their chain of threads.

Well, two days after purchasing Gay-Neck, his new owner came to me and said, "Gay-Neck has run away."

"How?" I asked.

"I don't know, but I cannot find him in my house."

"Did you tie his wings? Could he fly?" I asked.

"His wings were tied," he answered.

That struck terror to my soul. I said: "Oh, you brother of a camel and cousin of an ass, instead of running hither, you should have sought for him in your own neighborhood. Do you not see that he tried to fly, but since his wings were tied, he fell off your roof? And by now he has been killed and devoured by some cat. Oh, this is a slaughter of a pigeon. You have robbed mankind of its diadem of carriers! You have murdered the glory of pigeon-hood!" Thus I reproached him.

My words frightened the man so thoroughly that he begged me to come with him and hunt for Gay-Neck. My first thought was to rescue the poor fellow from cats. We spent a whole afternoon, but in vain. I examined more sordid alleyways in twelve hours, expecting to find him at bay before some mangy cat, than I have done in all the rest of my life. Alas, he was not to be found. That night I came home late, for which I got a good scolding, and went to bed a broken-hearted boy.

My mother, who understood my state of mind, did not wish me to enter the world of sleep with hurt and excited feelings. She spoke: "Your pigeon is safe. Go to sleep in a calm mood."

"Why, Mother?"

She answered: "If you are calm, your tranquil thoughts can help you. If you are peaceful, your serenity will make him serene. And if he is serene, his mind will work well. And you know, my beloved, how keen Gay-Neck's mind is. If he sets to work with tranquillity he will overcome all obstacles and reach home and safety. Now let us make a prayer to Infinite Compassion, and calm ourselves." So we sat surrounded by the silence of night for half an hour, saying: "I am serene. All that exists is serene. Peace, peace, peace be unto all! Om Shanti, shanti, shanti!"

As I was going to sleep my mother said: "You will now dream no bad dreams. Now that God's peace and compassion are kindled in you, you will have a night of fruitful rest. Peace!"

That it proved to be fruitful there is no doubt. For about eleven in the morning, Gay-Neck flew up across the sky. He rode high. How he freed his

wings I shall have to tell you in his own language.
Let us again use the grammar of fancy and the dictionary of imagination.

"O master of many tongues," began Gay-Neck
on our own roof, "I could abide not more than a
day in that man's house! He gave me insect-infected
grain to eat, and made me drink water that was not
fresh. After all, I am a soul; why should I be treated
as a stone or shard? Moreover, he tied my wings
with evil-smelling fishing tackle. Would I stay with
such an one? Never! So hardly had he put me on the
white roof of his house and gone downstairs, than
I flapped my wings and flew. Alas! my wings were
heavy, and it hurt me to fly. So I fell on the awning
of a shop in the lane near by. There I sat waiting
and watching for help. I saw some swifts go by; I
called to them, but they were not my friends. I saw
a wild pigeon; I called, but he too made no response. Just then I beheld a dark cat coming towards me. Here was death on four feet. As it drew
nearer and nearer, its topaz eyes burned with red.
It crouched and made ready to spring. I, too, sprang
—clear over his head on to the cornice about five
feet above the awning, where a swift had made his
home. Though it was most difficult, I clung to that
spot until the black one vanished. Now I leaped
again. Four or five feet above me was the roof.
There I perched. But my wing hurt. In order to ease
my pain, I massaged the roots of my feathers. One

by one my beak pressed and rubbed them, and then something slipped. One small feather I had succeeded in pressing out of the grip of the fishing tackle, which stank exceedingly. I kept on rubbing and pressing the next feather, and, behold, it too was free. Oh, what a glorious feeling! Soon the entire wing was free. Just then the black cat re-appeared on the roof, but now I was able to fly about ten feet and I reached the cornice of a high building, where I found a convenient perch. Thence I watched the deadly cat. He crouched, and sprang upon the fishing tackle just shed from my wing. That told me a new story: it was the stench of the fishing tackle that had attracted him, and not me. Forthwith I began to bite and press the cord that bound my other wing. By the time I had freed half the feathers, night came on; and when I had thrown my last evil-smelling chain away from my wing, I was forced to await the dawn to fly home, for owls fly in the early twilight, and hawks come later, and I wished to have a safe path through the air. Now I am at home—I am hungry and thirsty."

The first thing I did with my new pigeons was to give them food and fresh water. I never let them drink the water they bathed in. Since Gay-Neck's wing smelt of fish, I gave him separate quarters from the other pigeons. It took three days longer and three good baths before Gay-Neck was fit for decent society. In passing, let me remark that my father made me return the money to the man who had bought Gay-Neck with such deplorable results. To tell you the truth, I did not wish to then. But now I feel I did right in obeying my parent. After a fortnight, and before unbinding the wings of my newly acquired pigeons, I bribed them to love me. Every morning I would put some millet seed and peanuts in ghee (clarified butter). After they had been soaked in butter all day, I gave a dozen each to every one of my pets. They were so fond of those delicacies that in two days' time they had formed the habit of coming to me before five in the afternoon, begging for buttered seeds. In three more days I freed their wings, in a subtle way, undoing them about fifteen minutes before five. They all flew off the moment they felt their liberty. But lo, after the first exhilaration of finding their freedom had passed, they flew down to the roof again for their meal of buttered peanuts and millet seeds! It is a pity that we have to win our pigeons' confidence by feeding their stomachs, but alas! I have noticed that there are many men and women who resemble pigeons in this respect!

War Training *(continued)*

THE NEW PIGEONS gradually learned to fly farther and farther away from the house as day followed day. At the end of a month they were taken a distance of fifty miles and more and uncaged, and with the exception of two who apparently fled home to their previous owner, all returned to me under Gay-Neck's leadership.

The question of an undisputed leadership was not an easy one to settle. In fact, a serious battle had to be fought out between Gay-Neck and two new males, Hira and Jahore. The last named was a pure-black tumbler. His feathers shone like panther's fur. He was gentle and not fierce, yet he refused to submit to Gay-Neck's leadership of the entire flock. You know how quarrelsome and full of display carriers generally are. On my roof all the carrier males used to strut, coo and talk as if each one of them was the monarch of all he surveyed. If Gay-Neck thought himself Napoleon, Hira (Diamond), the white carrier—as white "as the core of sunlight," to express it poetically—considered himself Alexander the Great, while Jahore (Black Diamond), though not a carrier, let it be known that he was Julius Caesar and Marshal Foch rolled into one. Besides those three, there were other conceited males, but they had already been beaten in battle by one or the other of the above three. Now it was necessary to fight out the question of absolute leadership of the entire flock.

One day Hira was seen preening his wings and talking nonsense in the presence of *Mrs.* Jahore, a beautiful jet-black creature with eyes as red as bloodstone. Matters had hardly gone any distance when from nowhere came Jahore, and fell upon Hira. The latter was so infuriated that he fought like a fiend. Beak against beak, feet against feet, and wings pitted against wings. All the other pigeons fled from the ring where the two males were engaged in trouncing each other. Gay-Neck stood over them, calm as an umpire over a tennis match. At last, after half a dozen set-tos, Hira won. Puffing himself to the uttermost limits of his conceit, he went over to *Mrs.* Jahore as much as to say: "Madame, your husband is a coward. Behold what a fine fellow I am. Buk, bukoom, kumkum." She gave him one crushing look of contempt, and flapping her wings withdrew to her husband in their home. Hira looked crestfallen and sulky in turn; then in a sudden paroxysm of anger he fell upon Gay-Neck tooth and nail. The latter, taken unaware, was very nearly knocked out at the first fury of the attack. Hira pecked and slapped him till he felt too dizzy to stand up, so Gay-Neck ran away pursued by the mad fellow. They ran in a circle, spinning like two tops. I could hardly see which was pursuer and which pursued. They went at such high speed that I could not see when they stopped and started to peck and slap each other. The explosive sound of wing hitting wing filled the air with an ominous clamour. Now feathers began to fly in every direction. Suddenly, beak to beak and claw in claw they wrestled and spun on the floor—two birds become a single incarnation of fury. Seeing that they could not reach any decision that way, Gay-Neck extricated himself from his rival's grip and flew up in the air. Hira followed, flapping his wings tremendously fast. About three feet above the ground Gay-Neck put his claws like talons around Hira's windpipe, and set to squeezing it more and more tightly, and at the same time kept up a terrific cannonade of wing-beats that, like flails of steel, threshed out a shower of snowy feathers from his opponent's body. Now, hid in that falling blizzard of feathers, the two rolled on the ground, pecking each other with the virulence of two maddened serpents. At last Hira let go and wilted like a torn white flower on the floor. One of his legs had been dislocated. As for Gay-Neck, his throat and neck had hardly any feathers left. But he was glad that the struggle had been settled one way or another. And he knew full well that had Hira not first expended half his strength fighting Jahore, he, Gay-Neck, might not have won the battle. However, all is well that ends well. I bandaged and did all that was necessary to Hira's leg. In another thirty minutes all the pigeons were eating their last meal of the day, utterly oblivious of what had happened so recently. No sulking and bearing of grudges in their blood—no doubt they all came from a fine set of ancestors! Good breeding prevailed even among the smallest of them, and needless to add, Hira took his defeat like a gentleman.

By now January had come, with cool weather and clear skies, and the competition for pigeon prizes began. Each man's flock was tested on three points: namely, team-work, long-distance flight and flight under danger. We won the first prize on the first point, but I am sorry to say that owing to a sad mishap which you shall learn of in its proper place, my pigeons could not compete for the other two.

This is the nature of the team-work competition. The various flocks of pigeons fly way up from their respective homes. Once they are beyond the reach of whistling and other sounds that indicate their master's voice, the diverse flocks coalesce. Then spontaneously they agree to fly under the leadership of a pigeon whom they consider fit. All this happens up in the air where pigeon-wit and pigeon-instinct prevail, and the bird who flies forward and is allowed to lead does so without ever realizing the nature and the reason of the honour that has been bestowed on him.

The temperature dropped to forty-five. It was a fine cold morning for our part of India, in fact the coldest day of the year. The sky above, as usual in the winter, was cloudless and remote, a sapphire intangibility. The city houses—rose, blue, white and yellow—looked like an army of giants rising from the many-coloured abyss of dawn. Far off, the horizons burned in a haze of dun and purple. Men and women in robes of amber and amethyst, after having said their morning prayers to God, were raising their arms from the house-tops in gestures of benediction to the rising sun. City noises and odours were unleashed from their kennels of the night. Kites and crows were filling the air with their cries. Over the din and clamour one could yet hear the song of the flute-players. At that moment the signal whistle blew that the contest had begun, and each pigeon-fancier waved from his roof a white flag. Instantly from nowhere innumerable flocks of pigeons rose into the sky. Flock upon flock, colour upon colour, their fluttering wings bore them above the city. Crows and kites—the latter of two species, red and brown—fled from the sky before the thundering onrush of tens of thousands of carriers and tumblers. Soon all the flocks—each flying in the shape of a fan—circled in the sky like so many clouds caught in large whirlpools of air. Though each moment they ascended higher, for a long time each owner of a flock knew his own from the others; and even when at last the separate flocks merged into a single unit and flew like a solid wall of wings, I could pick out, by the way they flew, Gay-Neck, Hira, Jahore and half a dozen others. Each bird had personal characteristics that marked him as he flew. When any owner wished to call the attention of any one of his pigeons, he blew a shrill whistle with certain stops as a signal. That attracted the bird's attention if he was within reach of the sound.

At last the whole flock reached such a height that not even the blast of a trumpet from any pigeon-fancier could reach it. Now they stopped circling in the air and began to move horizontally. The competition for leadership had begun. As they manoeuvred from one direction of the heavens to another, we, the owners below, had to look up intently in order to make sure of the characteristics of the one whom the pigeons had trusted to lead their flight.

For a moment it looked as if my Jahore would lead. But hardly had he gone to the head of the flock when they all turned to the right. That brought about a confusion in the ranks, and, like horses on a race-course, all kinds of unknown pigeons pushed forward. But in time each one of them was pushed back by the rest of the flock. This happened so often that we began to lose interest in the contest. It looked as though some nondescript pigeon would win the coveted leadership prize.

Now suddenly rose the cry from many house-tops: "Gay-Neck, Gay-Neck, Gay-Neck!" Yes, many of the pigeon-fanciers were shouting that name. Now I could see—without the slightest shadow of error —my own bird at the head of that vast flock—a leader among leaders—directing their manoeuvres. Oh, what a glorious moment! He led them from horizon to horizon, each time rising a few feet higher, till by eight in the morning not a pigeon could be seen in any corner of the sky. Now we furled our flags and went downstairs to study our lessons. At midday, when again we went above, each man could see the entire wall of pigeons descending. Lo! Gay-Neck was still leading. Again rose the shout "Gay-Neck, Gay-Neck!" Yes, he had won the palm, for he had remained in leadership for more than four hours, and was coming down as he had gone up— a master!

Now came the most dangerous part of the flight.

The Commander of the vast concourse gave the order to disband, and flock after flock split from the main body, each separate flock flying away to its home. But not too quickly. Some must guard the sky above them while the others flew homeward. Gay-Neck held my little flock in a kind of umbrella formation to protect the rear of the receding pigeons belonging to other contestants. Such is the price of leadership—the other name of self-sacrifice.

But now began a horrible climax. In India during the winter the buzzards called Baz come south. They do not eat carrion; like the eagle and the hawk the Baz generally eats what he kills with his own talons. They are mean and cunning—I think they are a class of low-born eagles—but they resemble kites, although their wings are not frayed at the ends. They fly in pairs slightly above a flock of kites and are hidden by them from their prey, which, however, they can see in this way without ever being seen themselves.

On that particular day, just when Gay-Neck had won the leader's laurels, I perceived a pair of Baz flying with a flock of kites. Instantly I put my fingers in my mouth and blew a shrill whistle. Gay-Neck understood my signal. He redistributed his followers, he himself leading the centre, while Jahore and Hira he ordered to cover the two ends of the crescent, in which shape the flock was flying. The entire group held together as though it were one vast bird. They

then began to dip down faster and faster. By now
the task for which they tarried in the heavens was
done. All the other flocks that they had played
with in the morning had gone home.

Seeing them dip down so fast, a Baz fell in front
of them like a stone dropping from a Himalayan
cliff. Just when he had descended to the level of my
birds, he opened his wings and faced them. This was
no new tactic, for it has been used in the past by
every Baz in order to strike terror into a flock of
pigeons. That it succeeds in ten cases out of eleven
is undeniable, for when it happens the terror-struck
pigeons lose their sense of solidarity and fly pell-mell
in every direction. No doubt that was what the Baz
hoped for now; but our wily Gay-Neck, beating his
wings, flew without a tremor under the enemy about
five feet, drawing the whole flock after him. He
did it, knowing that the enemy never pounces upon
a solidly unified group. But hardly had he gone a
hundred yards forward when the second, probably
Mrs. Baz, fell in front of the pigeons and opened
her wings as her husband had done. But Gay-Neck
paid no attention. He led the whole flock straight
toward her. It was inconceivable. No pigeon had
dared do that before, and she fled from their attack.
Hardly had her back been turned when Gay-Neck
and the rest of the pigeons dipped and swooped as
fast as they could go. By now they were hardly six
hundred feet from our roof, and then, as fate would

have it, Mr. Baz, like a shell full of high explosives, fell again, this time right in the middle of the crescent, and opened his wings and beak like forks of fire, crying and shrieking with fury. That produced its effect. Instead of one solid wall of pigeons, the flock was cut in two, of which one half followed Gay-Neck, while the other, smitten with abject fear, flew none knew whither. Gay-Neck did what a true leader does in great crises. He followed that panic-stricken flock until his section overtook it, and in no time, lo, they had merged into a single group once more. Hardly had that taken place when Mrs. Baz in her turn descended like a thunderbolt between him and the other pigeons. She almost fell on his tail, and cut him off from the rest, who now, deprived of their mentor, sought safety in flight, paying no heed to anything. That isolated Gay-Neck completely, and exposed him to attacks from every side. Still undaunted, he tried to fly down to his retreating followers. Ere he had descended a dozen feet, down before him swooped Mr. Baz. Now that Gay-Neck saw the enemy so near, he grew more audacious, and tumbled. It was a fortunate action. Had he not done so, Mrs. Baz, who had shot out her talons from behind, would have captured him then and there.

In the meantime the rest of my pigeons were beating on, and had almost reached home. They were falling on the roof as ripe fruits fall from a tree.

But one among them was not a coward. On the contrary, he was of the very essence of bravery. It was Jahore, the black diamond. As the whole crowd settled down on our roof, he tumbled and flew higher. There was no mistake about his intentions. He was going to stand by Gay-Neck. Seeing him tumble again, Mr. Baz changed his mind. He gave up pursuing Gay-Neck and swooped down after Jahore. Well, you know Gay-Neck—he dipped to the rescue of Jahore—circling and curving as swiftly as a coil of lightning, leading Mrs. Baz panting after him. She could not make as many curves as Gay-Neck, no, not nearly so many. But Mr. Baz, who was a veteran, had flown up and up to take aim; this put Jahore in danger. One more wrong turn, and Mr. Baz would have him. Alas! poor bird; he did the thing he should not have done. He flew in a straight line below Mr. Baz, who at once shut his wings and fell like a thunderclap of Silence. No noise could be heard, not even "the shadow of a sound." Down, down, down, he fell, the very image of death. Then the most terrible thing happened. Between him and Jahore slipped, none knew how, Gay-Neck, in order to save the latter and frustrate the enemy. Alas! instead of giving up the attack, the Baz shot out his talons, catching a somewhat insecure hold of the intruder. A shower of feathers covered the air. One could almost see Gay-Neck's body writhing in the enemy's grip. As if a hot iron had gone through me, I shrieked with pain for my bird! But nothing availed. Round and round, higher and higher that Baz carried him, trying to get a more secure hold with his talons. I must admit something most humiliating here. I had been so intent on saving Gay-Neck that I did not notice when Mrs. Baz fell and captured Jahore. It must have happened very swiftly, right after Gay-Neck was caught. Now the air was filled with Jahore's feathers. The enemy held him fast in her talons, and he made no movement to free himself. But not so Gay-Neck; he was still writhing in the grip of Mr. Baz. As if to help her husband to grasp his prey more securely, Mrs. Baz flew very close to her lord. Just then Jahore struggled to get free. That swung her so near that her wing collided with her husband's. The fellow lost his balance. As he was almost overturned in the air, with another shower of feathers Gay-Neck wrenched himself free from his grip. Now he dropped down, down, down. . . . In another thirty seconds a panting, bleeding bird lay on our roof. I lifted him up in order to examine his wound. His two sides were torn, but not grievously. At once I took him to the pigeon doctor, who dressed his wounds. It took about half an hour, and when I returned home and put Gay-Neck in his nest, I could not find Jahore anywhere. His nest, alas, was empty. And when I went up to the roof, there I found Jahore's wife sitting on the parapet, scanning every direction of the sky for a sign of her husband. Not only did she spend that day, but two or three more in the same manner. I wonder if she found any consolation in the fact that her husband sacrificed himself for the sake of a brave comrade.

Mating of Gay-Neck

GAY-NECK'S wounds healed very slowly. Until about the middle of February he could not be made to fly more than ten yards above the roof. The duration of his flight, too, was very short. No matter how frequently I chased him off the roof, I could not keep him in the air more than a quarter of an hour. At first I thought that it was his lungs that were out of order. When, after investigation, they proved sound, I ascribed his disinclination to fly to his heart, which might have been injured by his latest mishap. That assumption also proved erroneous after a second investigation.

So, utterly exasperated by Gay-Neck's behaviour,

I wrote a long letter to Ghond describing everything that had happened. It turned out that he had gone on a hunting-trip with some Englishmen. Receiving no help from that quarter, I decided to examine my pigeon most closely. Day after day I put him on our house-top, and watched, but no clue was vouchsafed me as to the nature of his trouble. So I gave up all hope of seeing Gay-Neck fly again.

About the end of February I received a cryptic note from Ghond from the deeps of the jungle. It read: "Your pigeon is frightened. Cure him of his fear. Make him fly." But he did not say how. Nor could I devise anything that would make Gay-Neck wing his way into the higher spaces. It was no use chasing him off the roof, for if I chased him off one corner, he flew across to another and perched there. And what was most disconcerting was that if the shadow of a cloud or a flock of birds flying in the sky fell on him on our roof, he would tremble with terror. Doubtless every shadow that fell filled his mind with the feeling that it was a Baz or a falcon swooping down on him. That gave me an idea of how badly shaken Gay-Neck was. How to cure him of his disease of fear proved most baffling. Had we been in the Himalayas, I would have taken him to the holy man who once healed him of a similar ailment, but here in the city there was no lama. I was forced to wait.

March had ushered in spring, and Gay-Neck,

who had gone through an unusual moulting, looked like the very heart of a deep and large aquamarine. He was beautiful beyond description. One day, I know not how, I found him talking to Jahore's widow. She looked very bright with the advent of spring. In the sunlight her black-opal complexion glowed like a tropical night shot with stars. Of course I knew that marriage between her and Gay-Neck, though not the best thing for their offspring, might win him from his fear and her from the morose temper that had grown upon her ever since Jahore died.

In order to encourage their friendship, I took the two together in a cage to my friend Radja, who lived on the edge of the jungle about two hundred miles away. The name of his village was Ghatsila. It stood on the bank of a river across which lay high hills densely forested and full of all kinds of animals. Radja, being the priest of the village, which office his ancestors had held for ten centuries, and his parents were housed in a large building of concrete. The village temple, also of concrete, was adjacent to the house. In the courtyard of the temple, surrounded by high walls, Radja every night performed the duty of reading the Scriptures and explaining them to the peasantry that assembled there. While he would read aloud inside, outside would come from far off the yell of a tiger or the trumpeting of wild elephants across the narrow river. It

was a beautiful and sinister place. Nothing dangerous happened in the village of Ghatsila, but you did
not have to go very far to encounter any beast of
prey that you cared to seek.

The train that brought me there reached Ghatsila
at night. Radja and two servants of his house greeted
me at the station. One of the servants took my bundle on his shoulder, and the other carried the cage
with the two pigeons. Each of us had to carry a
hurricane-proof lantern, an extra one having been
brought for me. In single file, one servant leading
and another in the rear, we walked for an hour.
My suspicions were aroused, and I asked, "Why do
we go round about?"

Radja said: "In the spring wild animals pass
through here going north. We can't take short cuts
through the woods."

"Nonsense!" I exclaimed. "I have done it many
times before. When do we reach home?"

"In half an hour—"

Then, as if the very ground had opened at our
feet and belched out a volcano with a terrific noise,
arose the cry "Hoa—ho—ho—ho—hoa!"

The pigeons fluttered their wings in panic in their
cage. I gripped Radja's shoulder with my disen-
gaged hand, but instead of sharing my feelings he
laughed out loud. And—like master like servant—
the two servants laughed too.

After their mirth had subsided, Radja explained:

"You have done this many times, have you? Then why did the cry of monkeys frightened by lanterns scare you?"

"Monkeys?" I questioned.

"Yes, lots of them," my friend reminded me, "go north this time of the year. We frightened a whole flock in the trees overhead. That's all. In the future don't take every monkey yell for the roar of a tiger."

Fortunately, we reached home shortly, without any other incident to upset my complacency.

The next morning Radja went to his duties at his ancestral temple, while I sought the roof and un-caged my birds. At first they were bewildered, but seeing me near them with my hands full of but-tered seeds, they settled down to breakfast without any ado. Pretty nearly all of that day we spent on the roof. I dared not leave them by themselves very long lest the strangeness of their surroundings upset them.

In the course of the week that followed, the two birds made themselves at home in Ghatsila, and moreover became extremely intimate with each other. There was no doubt now that I had acted wisely in isolating them from the rest of the flock. About the eighth day of our stay, Radja and I were surprised to see Gay-Neck fly in pursuit of his mate. She flew on, but at a low altitude. He followed. See-ing him catch up to her, she rose and turned back. He too did the same, and followed after. Again she

*No beast of prey can kill his victim without frighten-
ing him first.   page 128*

rose. But this time he balked, and began to circle the air beneath her. However, I felt that he was regaining his confidence. At last Gay-Neck, the paragon of pigeons, was healing himself of his fear and of his horror of the heavens; he was once more at home in the sky.

The next morning the birds flew higher and played with each other. Gay-Neck again refused to go all the way, and began to come down hastily instead of circling in the air below her. That puzzled me, but Radja, who was a keen person, explained. "A cloud, large as a fan, has come over the sun. Its shadow fell so suddenly that Gay-Neck thought it was his enemy. Wait until the cloud passes, and then—"

Radja was right. In a few more seconds the sun came out and its light dripped from Gay-Neck's wings once more. At once he stopped coming downwards and began to make circles in the air. His mate too, who had been coming down to keep him company, waited for him a hundred feet or so above. Now Gay-Neck rose, beating his wings like an eagle freed from his cage. The sunlight made pools of colour about him as he swerved and swung up and up. Soon, instead of following, he led his mate. Thus they ascended the sky—he healed of fear completely, and she ravished by his agility and power.

The next morning both of them made an early start. They flew far and very long. For a while they were lost beyond the mountains, as if they had slid over their peaks and down the other side. They were gone at least an hour.

At last they returned about eleven o'clock, each bearing in his beak a large straw. They were going to build a nest for the laying of eggs. I thought I would take them home, but Radja insisted that we should stay at least a week longer.

Every day during that week we spent some hours in the more dangerous jungle across the river, taking the two pigeons with us in order to release them in the dense forest hardly five miles from Radja's house. Gay-Neck forgot everything save testing his sense of direction and making higher flights. In other words, love for his mate and the change of place and climate healed him of fear, that most fell disease.

Here let it be inscribed in no equivocal language that almost all our troubles come from fear, worry and hate. If any man catches one of the three, the other two are added unto it. No beast of prey can kill his victim without frightening him first. In fact, no animal perishes until its destroyer strikes terror into its heart. To put it succinctly, an animal's fear kills it before its enemy gives it the final blow.

War Calls Gay-Neck

BY THE FIRST WEEK of August, just after the children were born, Hira and Gay-Neck had gone from Calcutta to Bombay, setting sail with Ghond to serve in the World War. I sent that bachelor bird Hira with Gay-Neck because the army had need of both.

I was very glad that Gay-Neck had some knowledge of his little ones before he sailed for the battlefield of Flanders and France. The chief reason for this happiness was that I knew that a pigeon whose wife and new-born children are waiting at home rarely fails to return. That bond of love between Gay-Neck and his family assured me that he would do his work of carrying messages very well. No sound of gun-fire, nor bullets, as long as he lived, could keep him from returning home at the end.

But here one may raise the question that home was in Calcutta and the war was thousands of miles away. That is true. But all the same, because he had left his wife and children at home, he would do his utmost to fly back to his temporary nest with Ghond.

It is said that Gay-Neck carried several important messages between the front and General Headquarters where the Commander-in-Chief and Ghond waited for him. Of course, Gay-Neck was attached to Ghond first. But in the course of the following months he became very fond of the Chief.

Ghond and not I went to the front with the two pigeons, for I was under age and ineligible for any kind of service, so the old fellow had to take them. During the voyage out from India to Marseilles, Hira and Gay-Neck and the old hunter became fast friends. I have yet to see any strange animal resist Ghond's friendship long, and since my pigeons had known him before, it was easy for them to respond to him.

During the stay of the Indian Army in Flanders from September 1914 till the following spring, Ghond remained near General Headquarters with his cage, while Hira or Gay-Neck was taken by different units to the front. There from time to time messages were written on thin paper weighing no more than an ounce, and were tied to his feet; then he was released. Gay-Neck invariably flew to Ghond at the General Headquarters of the army. There the message was deciphered and answered by the Commander-in-Chief himself. It is rumoured that the latter personage loved Gay-Neck, and valued his services highly.

But it is better to listen to Gay-Neck's own story. As the experiences of a dream cannot be told except by the dreamer, so some of the adventures of Gay-Neck he should recount in person.

"After we crossed the black water—the Indian Ocean and the Mediterranean—we travelled by rail through a very strange country. Though it was September, yet that country—France—was as cold as southern India in the winter. I expected to see snow-capped mountains and giant trees, for I thought I was nearing the Himalayas. But no hills higher than our tallest bamboo trees could I perceive on the horizon. I do not see why a land has to be cold when it is not high.

"At last we reached the battle-front. It turned out to be the rear end of it, but even there you could hear the boom, boom, boom of the fire-spitters. And, as a normal pigeon, I hate all fire-spitters no matter of what size and shape. Those metal dogs barking and belching out death were not to my liking. After I had been there a couple of days, our trial flight began. There were only four pigeons of our own city besides Hira and myself. You know how rash

Hira could be. No sooner had we flown up above the houses of a large village than Hira flew towards the direction of the boom, boom, boom. He wanted to investigate. Well, in an hour's time we were there. Oh, what a noise! Big balls of fire, spat out like thunderbolts by the metal dogs hidden under trees, hissed and exploded below us. I was frightened, so I rose higher and higher. But no peace there in the highest heavens could I find. From nowhere came vast eagles roaring and growling like trumpeting elephants. At such a terrific sight, we flew towards where Ghond was waiting for us. But the eagles, two of them, followed! We went faster and faster. Fortunately, they could not overtake us. Just as we had expected, those eagles came down where we lived. I felt death was at hand. Those eagles were going to devour us in our cages like weasels. But no! They stopped trumpeting soon and lay down on the field—dead. Two men each jumped out of the stomachs of those two birds and walked away. I wondered how eagles could devour human beings. And how could the fellows come out alive?

"Soon enough the men returned from their errand, climbed inside the eagles, and then with a groan and trumpeting racket, they came alive and flew up in the air again. That left no doubt in my mind that they were men's chariots, and when I knew that I felt relieved.

"Though everything looked strange at first, it

ceased to be so after we got used to it; yet the problem of sleeping soundly under the continual booming and barking noises remained unsolved. All those months in the army I never slept well. No wonder Hira and I were nervous and fidgety, like newly hatched snakes.

"My first adventure consisted of taking a message from the Rasseldar at the front where all kinds of dogs barked and spat fire day and night. I must tell you a word about the Rasseldar. He was in charge of a lot of Indian warriors from Calcutta. He took me in a cage completely covered with black canvas, and with his forty men set out for the front trench. After going for hours and nights—for that is what it felt like in my darkened cage—we reached our destination. There the canvas was removed. Now I could see nothing but walls around me where turbaned men from India crawled like little insects. Overhead flew the mechanical eagles trumpeting with terror. Here for the first time I began to grasp sounds. Instead of one confused boom, boom, boom, there were as many grades of explosion as the ear could distinguish. The hardest one to make out was the talk of the men about me. Under the deafening sounds their talk sounded like the whisper of a lazy breeze in the grass. Now and then they unmuzzled a metal dog that barked—spitting out fire for a long stretch of time. Then came the laughter of a hyena. Hundreds of men goaded those little pups to an

That sound was drowned in the deep-toned cry of the eagles above who screeched like mad, slaying each other. page 139

awful coughing—puck puff, puck puff, puck puff!
That sound was drowned in the deep-toned cry of
the eagles above who flew in flocks and barked as
well as screeched like mad, slaying each other like
so many sparrows. The Rasseldar who was in charge
of me pointed the face of his pup at the sky, then
let off—puck puff—some fire, and lo! it brought
down one of those eagles as if it were a rabbit. Now
the deepest tone was heard. The boom bazoom bum
bum! The tiger-roar of the large ones' mammoth
majesty rose and spread like a canopy of divine
chords, drowning under its engulfing immensity all
other petty sounds. Oh, the excruciating enchantment of that organ tone! Can I ever forget? Roar
upon roar, titanic tonality on tonality, like cata-
clysmic boulders of sounds crashed and clamoured!

"Why does beauty lie so close to death? Hardly
had the ineffable glory of that supernal music overhead seized my soul when balls of fire fell about
us like a torrential rain. Men fell and succumbed
like rats in flooded holes. The Rasseldar, who was
bleeding and red, wrote hastily on a piece of paper,
tied it to my feet, and uncaged me. I knew by the
look in his eyes that he was in dire distress and
wanted Ghond to bring him succour.

"Of course you know, my master, I flew up; but
what I beheld almost froze my wings. The air above
the trenches was one sheet of flying fire. How to
rise above it was my problem. I used my tail-rudder,

and steered my flight in every direction. But no matter which way I rose, above me ran a million shuttles of flame, weaving the garment of red destruction on the loom of life. But I had to rise, I, Gay-Neck, the son of my father. And soon I struck a pocket of air that was full of a current that sucked and whirled me up as if my wing were broken and I were as light as a leaf. It turned me up and down and up again till I had torn my way through the fabric of fire that kept on weaving itself with ever-increasing rapidity. But I had no eye for anything now. 'To Ghond, to Ghond,' I kept saying to myself. Every time I said that, it dug like a fresh goad into my spirit and made me put forth my greatest effort. Now that I had risen very high, I made my observations and flew westwards. Just then a shot pierced and broke my rudder. Half of my tail was burned and torn away from me. And you know that made me furious! My tail is my point of honour. I can't bear it to be touched, let alone shot at. Well, I flew safely home, but just about the moment I was getting ready to do down, two eagles started a fight above me. I had not heard their trumpeting or seen their faces. Had they killed each other I would not have minded, but they let loose a hurricane of flames after me. The more they fought, the more fire fell from their beaks. I dived and ducked as well as I could. If only they had had some trees there. Of course, there had been trees, but most of them had been shot and mutilated so that they stuck out like stumps, with no shade-giving gracious foliage or any prodigious boughs. So I had to zigzag my way round and about those dilapidated spikes like a man fleeing from elephants in the jungle. At last I reached home and perched on Ghond's wrist. He cut the thread and took the message with me to the Commander-in-Chief, who looked like a ripe cherry and exuded a pleasant odour of soap. Probably, unlike most soldiers, he bathed and soaped himself clean three or four times a day. After he had read what was scribbled on that paper by the Rasseldar, he patted me on the head and grunted like a happy ox."

Second Adventure

"THE NEXT TIME we were taken to the front was after the Rasseldar recovered from his slight wounds. On this occasion he took both Hira and me. I knew at once that the message we were to carry was so important that two had to be trusted with it so that at least one might succeed.

"It was very cold. I felt as if I were living in a kingdom of ice. It rained all the time. The ground was so foul that every time you stepped on it your feet got caught in mud like quicksand, and your feet felt so cold, as if you had stepped on a corpse.

"Now we reached a strange place. It was not a trench, but a small village. Around it beat and burst the tides of burning destruction. It was, by the look on the men's faces, a very sacred and important place, for they did not want to give it up, though the red tongues of death licked almost every roof, wall and tree of this place. I was very glad to be in an open space. One could see the grey sky low, oh, so very low. And one could see the frost-whited patches of ground where no shell had yet fallen. Even there, in that very heart of pounding and shooting, where houses fell as birds' nests in tempests, rats ran from hole to hole, mice stole cheese, and spiders spun webs to catch flies. They went on with the business of their lives as if the slaughtering of men by their brothers were as negligible as the clouds that covered the sky.

"After a while the booming stopped. And it looked as if the village—that is, what was left of it—were safe from attack. It grew darker and darker. The sky lowered so far that I could put my beak into it. The dank cold seized every feather of my body and began to pull it out, as it were. I found it utterly impossible to sit still in our cage. Hira and I hugged each other tight in order to keep warm.

"Again firing broke out. This time from every direction. Our little village was an island surrounded by the enemy. Apparently under cover of the fog that had enwrapped everything, the enemy had cut off our connection from the rear. Then they started shooting the sky-rockets. It was dark and clammy like a Himalayan night, though it was hardly past noon. I wondered how men knew it was anything but night. Men, after all, know less than birds.

"Hira and I were released to carry our respective messages. We flew up, but not very far, for in a short time we were devoured by a thick fog. Our eyes could see nothing. A cold clammy film pressed itself on them, but I had anticipated something like this. I did what I would do under such circumstances, whether on a field of battle or in India. I flew upwards. It seemed as if I could go no farther than a foot at a time. My wings were wet. My breathing was caught in a long process of sneezing. I thought I should drop dead in an instant. Thank the Gods of the pigeons I could see for a few yards now! So I flew higher. Now my eyes began to smart. Suddenly I realized I must draw down my film—my second eyelids that I use in flying through a dust-storm—if I were to save myself from blindness, for we were not in a fog—it was an evil-smelling, eye-destroying smoke let out by men. My eyes pained as if somebody had stuck pins into them. My films now covered my eyes, and, holding my breath, I struggled upwards. Hira, who was accompanying me, rose too. He was choking to death with that gas. But he was not going to give up his flight. At last we rose clear of the sheet of poison smoke. The air was pure here, and as I removed the film from my eyes I saw, far away against the grey sky, our line. We flew towards it.

"Hardly had we flown half-way homeward when a terrible eagle with black crosses all over it flew nearer and spat fire at us—puck puff, puck puff, pop pa. . . . We ducked and did the best we could. We flew back to its rear. There the machine could not hit us. Imagine us flying over the tail of that machine-eagle. It could do nothing. It began to circle. So did we. It turned somersaults. So did we. It could do nothing without wriggling its tail; unlike that of a real eagle, its tail was as stiff as a dead fish. We knew that if we once came in front of it again, we would be killed instantaneously.

"Time was passing. I realized that we could not go on staying over the tail of that machine-eagle for ever. The village covered with poison gas that we had left behind held the Rasseldar and our friends. We must get our message through for their safety and succour.

"Just then the machine-eagle played a trick. It flew back towards its home. We did not wish to go into the enemy's line flying over its tail in order to be sniped by sharpshooters. Now that we were half-way to our own home and in sight of our line, we gave up being careful; we turned away from the machine-eagle and flew at our highest speed, rising higher every few wing-beats. No sooner had we done that than the miserable beast turned and followed. Fortunately, it took him a little time. There was no doubt now that we were flying over our own lines. Just the same that plane rose to our level and

kept on pouring fire on us—puff puff pop pa! Now
we were forced to duck and dive. I made Hira fly
under me. That protected him. So we flew, but fate
is fate. From nowhere came an eagle and fired at
the enemy. We felt so safe now that Hira and I flew
abreast of each other. Just then a bullet buzzed by
me and broke his wings. Poor wounded Hira! He
circled and fell through the air like a silver leaf, fortunately in our line. Seeing that he was dead, I flew
at lightning speed, never turning back to see the
duel of the two eagles.

"When I got home I was taken to the Commander-in-Chief. He patted my back. Then, for the
first time, I realized what an important message I
had brought, for as soon as the old man had read
the piece of paper he touched some queer ticking
things, and he lifted a piece of horn and growled
into it. Now Ghond took me to my nest. There, as
I perched, thinking of Hira, I felt the very earth
shake under me. Machine-eagles flew in the air as
thick as locusts. They howled, whirred and barked.
Below, from the ground, boomed and groaned innumerable metal dogs. Then came the deep-toned
howl of the big spitfires like a whole forest of tigers
gone mad. Ghond patted my head and said, 'You
have saved the day.' But there was no day in sight.
It was a darkening grey sky under which death
coiled and screamed like a dragon, and crushed all
in its grip. How bad it was you may gauge from

this: when I flew near our base for exercise next
morning I found that hardly a mile from my nest
the ground was ploughed up by shells. And even
rats and field-mice did not manage to escape: dozens
of them had been slaughtered and cut to pieces. Oh!
it was terrible. I felt so melancholy. Now that Hira
was dead I was alone, and so weary!"

Ghond Goes Reconnoitring

ABOUT THE FIRST week of December, Ghond and Gay-Neck were to go on a reconnaissance trip all by themselves. The place they went to was a forest not far from Ypres, Armentières and Hazebrouck. If you take a map of France and draw a line from Calais south almost in a straight line, you will come across a series of places where the British and Indian armies were situated. Near Armentières there are many graves of Indian Mohammedan soldiers. There are no graves of Indian Hindu soldiers because the Hindus from time immemorial have cremated their dead, and those that are cremated occupy no grave. Their ashes are scattered to the winds, and no place is marked or burdened with their memory.

To return to Ghond and Gay-Neck. They were
sent to a forest near Hazebrouck, which was behind
the enemy's line, to find out the exact location of
an enormous underground ammunition dump. If
found, Ghond and the pigeon, singly or together,
were to return to the British Army Headquarters
with an exact map of the place. That was all. So
one clear December morning, Gay-Neck was taken
on an aeroplane. It flew about twenty miles over a
forest, part of which was held by the Indian Army
and the rest by the Germans. When they had gone
beyond the German line, Gay-Neck was released.
He flew all over the woods; then, having gained
some knowledge of the nature of the land, he flew
back home. This was done to make sure that Gay-
Neck knew his route and had some inkling of what
was expected of him.

That afternoon when the sun had gone down,
which happened at about four o'clock at this lati-
tude ten degrees north of New York, Ghond, most
warmly dressed, with Gay-Neck under his coat,
started. They went on an ambulance as far as the
second line of the Indian Army in the great forest.
In utter darkness they proceeded to the front, con-
ducted by some members of the Intelligence Service.

Soon they found themselves in what is called No
Man's Land, but fortunately it was covered with
trees, most of which had not yet been destroyed by
shell-fire. Ghond, who did not know French or German and whose knowledge of English was confined

to three words, "yes," "no" and "very well," was now left to find a German ammunition dump in a forest, accompanied only by a pigeon fast asleep under his coat.

First of all he had to remind himself that he was in a country of the cold Himalayan climate where, during the winter, trees stood bare and the ground was covered with dry autumn leaves and frost. Since there was very little foliage on tree or sapling, concealment of himself proved not an easy task. The night was dark, and as cold as a corpse, but since he could see in the dark better than any living man, and because his sense of smell was as keen as the keenest of all animals, he knew how to steer his course in No Man's Land. Fortunately, that night the wind was from the east.

Edging his way between tree-trunks, he pushed forward as fast as possible. His nose told him minutes before their arrival that a company of Germans was passing his way. Like a leopard he crawled up a tree, and waited. They never heard even the flicker of a sound. Had it been daylight they would have found him, for his bare feet bled as he walked on the frost-stricken ground, leaving distinct marks behind.

Once he had a very close shave. As he went up a tree and sat on a branch to let a couple of German sentries pass below him, he heard someone whisper from a branch into his ear. He knew at once that it was a German sharpshooter. But he bent his head, and listened. The German said, "Guten nacht," then stepped over and slid down the tree. No doubt he had taken Ghond for one of his fellow-soldiers who had come to relieve him. After a while Ghond descended to the ground and followed the footprint of that German. Dark though it was, his bare feet could feel where the ground had been worn down by the feet of man. No difficult task that, for him.

At last he reached a place where a lot of men were bivouacking. He had to skirt around them softly, still pressing forward. He heard a strange noise right at his feet. He stopped and listened. No mistake, this was a familiar sound! He waited. The steps of an animal: Patter pat, patter-r-r! Ghond moved towards the sound, and a suppressed growl ensued. Instead of fear, joy gripped his heart. He who had spent nights at a time in the tiger-infested jungles of India was not to be deterred by the growl of a wild dog. Soon enough two red eyes greeted his vision. Ghond sniffed the air before him carefully as he stood there, and lo! he could not detect there was the slightest odour of man about that dog; the creature had gone wild. The dog, too, was sniffing the air to find out what kind of being he was facing, for Ghond did not exude the usual human odour of fear, and so the animal came forward and rubbed against him and sniffed vigorously. Fortunately, Ghond carried Gay-Neck above the dog's

nose, and the odour of the bird's presence was carried up by the wind, so the wild dog perceived in
the man before him nothing but a friendly fearless
fellow. He wagged his tail, and whined. Ghond, instead of patting his head with his hand, slowly put
it before the dog's eyes to see and smell. A moment
of suspense followed. Was the dog going to bite the
hand? Another moment passed. Then . . . the dog
licked it. He now whined with pleasure. Ghond
said to himself: "So this hunter's dog is without a
master. Probably his master is dead. The poor beast
has become as wild as a wolf. He lives by preying on
the food supply of the German Army, for it is evi-
dent he has not yet eaten any human flesh. So much
the better."

Ghond whistled softly, the call of all hunters of
all ages no matter in what country. It meant "Lead."
And the dog led. He skirted all the bivouacs of the
German soldiers as deftly as a stag slips by a tiger's
den. After hours of wandering, they reached their
destination. There was no mistake about it; Ghond
had found the very depot not only of munitions but
also of German food supplies. His leader, the wild
dog, went through a secret hole in the ground, then
after half an hour emerged with a large leg of veal
between his jaws. That it was bovine meat Ghond
could tell by its odour. The dog sat down to his
dinner on the frosty ground, while the man put on
his boots, which he had carried slung over his shoul-

der all night long, and then looked up and took observations. By the position of the stars he could tell where he was. He waited there some time.

Slowly the day began to break. He took a compass from his pocket. Yes, he felt quite sure that he could draw a map of the place. Just then the dog jumped up and grabbed Ghond's coat with his teeth. There was no doubt in the man's mind that the dog wanted to lead him on again. He ran ahead, and Ghond followed as fast. Soon they reached a spot so thickly covered with thorns and frozen vines that passage through it was possible only for an animal. The dog crawled under a lot of sharp thorns, and disappeared.

Now Ghond drew a diagram showing the position of the stars, and the exact position of his compass, and tied both to Gay-Neck's foot, and let him go. He watched the pigeon fly from tree to tree, resting on each for a minute or so, and preening his wings. Then he struck the message tied to his foot with his beak—probably he was making sure that it was securely tied—flew up to the top of the tallest tree, and sat there examining the lay of the land. That moment Ghond, who was looking up, felt something pull him. He looked down at his feet; the dog was dragging him to a hole under the thorns. Ghond bent low, low enough to follow his mentor's direction, but at that moment he heard the flutter of wings overhead, then the barking of rifles. He had no desire to get up and investigate whether Gay-Neck had been killed or not. He crawled down under the thorns till he felt as if his stomach were glued against his backbone, and both sewed tightly to the ground. He pushed and crawled till suddenly he slid down, falling about eight feet into a dark hole. It was pitch dark, but Ghond hardly noticed that at first, for he was occupied in rubbing his bruised head.

When finally he tried to discover where he was, he made out that he must be sitting on a frozen water-hole covered, like a thieves' den, by impenetrable thorn-bushes. Even in winter when no leaf clad the branches and vines overhead, the darkness in daytime was thick there. The dog was still with him, and had evidently dragged him there to safety. The poor beast was so happy to have a friend with him that he wanted to play by the hour with Ghond, but the latter, being sleepy, dozed off into perfect slumber in spite of the noise of the guns not very far away.

After about three hours the dog suddenly whined and then yelled as if he were stricken with madness, after which the earth rocked under terrific sounds of explosion. Unable to bear it, the animal kept tugging the sleeve of Ghond's coat. The detonations rose crescendo upon crescendo till the place where Ghond lay literally swayed like a cradle, but he would not leave his hiding. All he said to himself was: "O Gay-Neck, thou incomparable bird, how well thou hast done thy task! Already thou hast borne the message to the cherry-faced chief, and this is his thunderous reply. O thou pearl among winged creatures!" So on he mumbled while the bombs dropped by aeroplanes ignited the German munitions dump.

Then the dog, who had been trying to pull him away by the sleeve of his coat, whined and shivered like one in high fever, and that instant something sizzled through the air and fell near by with a thud. With a desperate yell the poor dog dashed out of his hiding-place. Ghond followed. But too late. For hardly had he crept half-way under the thorns when an ear-splitting explosion seemed to cut the ground from under him, and a violent pain pierced his shoulder. He felt borne up by some demoniac power and flung to the ground with great force. Scarlet diamonds of light danced before his eyes for a few moments, followed by quenching darkness.

An hour later when he regained consciousness the first thing that he became aware of was a sound of Hindustani voices. In order to hear his native language more distinctly, he tried to raise his head. That instant he felt a shooting pain like the sting of a thousand cobras. There was no doubt in his mind now that he had been hit and probably mortally wounded. All the same his soul rejoiced every time he heard Hindustani spoken near him, for that meant that Indian troops, and not the enemy, were in possession of the forest now. "Ah," he said to himself, "my task is accomplished. I can die in peace."

Gay-Neck Tells How He Carried the Message

"ALL THAT NIGHT preceding the eventful day I slept very little. Though I lay under his coat, Ghond had no knowledge that I was awake. You cannot sleep next to the heart of a man who runs like a stag, climbs trees like a squirrel or picks up strange dogs for company every half-hour. . . . Ghond's heart thumped so hard now and then that you might have heard it yards away. He did another thing that was not conducive to sleep at such close quarters; he breathed irregularly all that night. Sometimes he inhaled long breaths. Sometimes he breathed as fast as a mouse fleeing from a cat. I might as well have tried to sleep on a storm in the sky as under the coat of such a man.

"Then that dog! Shall I ever forget him? I was frightened when Ghond first annexed him, but he got no scent from my body, and the air that rose from below told me that somehow, like a clean-smelling ghost, he had come to befriend us. His footsteps I shall remember all my life. He walked as softly as a cat. He must have been a savage dog, for dogs that live in civilization are noisy. They cannot even walk quietly. Man's company is corrupting: every animal, excepting cats, becomes careless and noisy in human society. But that dog was quite wild. He walked without noise. He breathed without any sound. Then how did I know that he was there? It was that odour that came up from the ground and greeted my nostrils.

"After a sleepless and most uncomfortable night Ghond let me go, and I could hardly recognize the place where he had released me. So I flew from tree to tree to find my bearings, which only drove fright into my very soul. For now that day had broken, the trees were filling up with eyes. Strange blue eyes were looking through tubes in different directions. There were men behind them, and one was looking from a tree-top about a foot from where I perched. He had not heard my coming, on account of all those metal dogs barking around us—puff papapa-pack!

"But as I flew up, he saw me. I felt that if I did not make haste and hide under other trees he would shoot me; and he did fire many times, but I was behind a copse as thick as the matted hair of a hermit. I decided to hop from tree to tree, not flying until the prospect was free of danger. I spent no little time in going about half a mile that way. At last my feet felt very fatigued, and I decided to fly, danger or no danger.

"Fortunately, no one had seen me fly up. I rose high after making large circles in the air. From a place whence the forest of trees appeared as small as saplings, I looked in different directions. Far off in the east, like chariots of gold, flew a flock of aeroplanes against the dawning sky. That meant the enemy's coming upon me if I waited much longer. So I started westwards. That seemed to be the signal for a thousand sharpshooters on tree-tops to fire at me.

"I think that when I circled up and above their trees, the Germans were uncertain whether I was their carrier or not, but the moment the sharpshooters perceived that I was going west they were sure that I was not their messenger, and so they shot at me to bring me down and find out what I carried on my foot.

"I could not go up for ever in the clear winter air without being frozen, and anyway, I did not want those enemy planes to gain on me. Again I dashed westwards, and again the wall of bullets spread before me like barbs of death. But I had no choice left; either pierce my way through, or be killed by the oncoming aeroplanes, who were so near that I could see their passengers. So I dashed towards the west. Fortunately, by now my tail, which was hurt about a month ago, had grown almost to its normal size. Without that rudder my task would have been twice as hard. As I kept on going towards our line, the fusillade increased. There was no doubt now that all the sharpshooters and men in the trenches far off were taking a shot at me. But I zigzagged, circled, tumbled and in fact did all the stunts and tricks I knew to cheat the ever-augmenting swarm of bullets, but all that zigzagging business lost me time. One of the aeroplanes had come within striking distance of even so small a mark as I made, and began to pour loads of fire from above and behind. There was nothing to do but go forward, so I dashed on. Oh! how hard I flew—fast as the fastest storm. Then—ftatattafut—I was hit! My leg was broken right near the groin, and it, with its message, dangled under me like a sparrow in a single talon of a hawk. Oh! the pain, but I had no time to think of that, for that aeroplane was still after me, and I flew harder than before.

"At last our own line came into view. I fled lower. The machine dived down too. I tried to tumble, but failed. My leg prevented me from trying any of my tricks. Then pa-pa-pat-pattut—my tail was hit, and a shower of feathers fell below, obscuring for a moment the view of the men in the German trenches. So I shot down in a slanting flight towards our line and—passed it, making a circle. Then I beheld a strange sight—the aeroplane had been hit by our men. It swayed, lurched, and fell. But it had done its worst ere it went down in flames—it had hit my right wing and broken it. It gave me satisfaction to see it catch fire in the air and fall, yet my own pain had increased so that I felt as if twenty buzzards were tearing me to pieces, but, thanks to the Gods of my race, I lost consciousness of either pain or pleasure, and felt as if a mountainous weight were pulling me down. . . .

"They kept me at the pigeon hospital for a month. Though my wing was repaired and my leg sewn up where it belonged, they could not make me fly again. Every time I hopped up in the air my ears, I know not how, were filled with terrible noises of guns, and my eyes saw nothing but flaming bullets. I was so frightened that I would dash immediately to the ground. You may say that I was hearing imaginary guns and seeing imaginary walls of bullets: maybe, but their effect on me was the same as that of real ones. My wings were paralysed, my entrails frozen with terror.

"Besides, I would not fly without Ghond. Why should I spring from the hands of a man whose complexion was not brown and whose eyes were blue? I had not known such people before. We pigeons don't take to any and every outsider. At last they brought me in a cage to the hospital where Ghond was, and left me beside him. When I saw him I hardly recognized him, for his eyes—Ghond's eyes —wore a look of real fear! Yes, he too had been frightened out of his wits for once. I know, as all birds and beasts do, what fear looks like, and I felt sorry for Ghond.

"But on seeing me, that film of terror left his eyes, and they burned with a light of joy. He sat up in bed, took me in his hands and kissed my foot that had held the message that he had sent. Then he patted my right wing, and said: 'Even in great distress, O thou constellation of divine feathers, thou hast borne thy owner with his message among friends and won glory for all pigeons and the whole Indian Army.' Again he kissed my foot. His humility touched me and by example humbled me. I felt no more pride when I remembered how I fell in the trenches of an Indian brigade after that aeroplane had partly smashed my wing, for had I fallen in a German trench, then . . . they would have seized the message on my leg; they would have surrounded the forest where Ghond lay hid with that wild dog—I shuddered to think of what they would have done! Alas! the dog, our true friend and saviour, where was he now?"

Healing of Hate and Fear

"THAT DOG," GHOND took up the story, "must have lost his French master early in the war. Probably the Germans had shot the man, and after that, when he saw his master's home looted and the barn set on fire, he went wild with terror and ran away into the woods, where he lived hidden from the sight of men under the thick thorn-bush, as spacious as a hut and as dark as the interior of a tomb. Probably he ventured out only at night in quest of food, and being a hunting-dog by heredity, all his savage qualities returned as he spent day after day and night after night in the woods like an outlaw.

"When he came across me, he was surprised because I was not afraid. I gave out no odour of fear. I must have been the first man in months whose fear did not frighten him to attack.

"Of course, he thought that, like himself, I too was hungry and was looking for food. So he led me to the German food depot, and through an underground passage he crawled into a vast provision chamber—a very gold-mine of food—and fetched some meat for me. I drew the conclusion that there were a series of underground chambers in which the Germans kept not only food but also oil and explosives, and I acted accordingly. Thank the Gods it turned out to be correct. Let us change the subject.

"To tell you the truth I hate to talk about the war. Look, the sunset is lighting the peaks of the Himalayas. The Everest burns like a crucible of gold. Let us pray:

> " 'Lead me from the unreal to the Real,
> From darkness into Light,
> From sound into Silence.' "

After meditation was over, Ghond silently walked out of our house to begin a journey from Calcutta to the lamasery near Singalila. But before I recount his adventure there, I must tell the reader how Ghond happened to be transferred from the battlefields of France to our home.

The last part of February 1915, it became quite clear to the Bengal Regiment that Gay-Neck would fly no more. Ghond, who had brought him, was no soldier. With the exception of a tiger or a leopard, he had never killed anything in his life, and now that he too was sick, they were both invalided back to India together. They reached Calcutta in March. I could not believe my eyes when I saw them. Ghond looked as frightened as Gay-Neck, and both of them appeared very sick.

Ghond, after he had delivered my pigeon to me, explained a few matters, before he departed to the Himalayas. "I need to be healed of fear and hate. I saw too much killing of man by man. I was in-valided home for I am sick with a fell disease—sickness of fear, and I must go alone to nature to be cured of my ill."

So he went up to Singalila, to the lamasery, there to be healed by prayer and meditation. In the mean-time I tried my utmost to cure Gay-Neck. His wife and full-grown children failed to help him. His chil-dren saw in him but a stranger, for he showed no care for them, but his wife interested him intensely, though even she could not make him fly. He refused steadily to do anything but hop a little, and nothing would induce him to go up in the air. I had his wings and legs examined by good pigeon-doctors, who said that there was nothing wrong with him. His bones and both his wings were sound, yet he would not fly. He refused even to open his right wing; and whenever he was not running or hopping he developed the habit of standing on one foot.

I would not have minded that, if he and his wife had not set about nesting just then. Towards the middle of April, when vacation for the hot weather began, I received Ghond's letter. "Your Gay-Neck," he informed me, "should not nest yet. If there are eggs, destroy them. Do not let them hatch under any circumstances. A sick father like Gay-Neck—diseased with fright—cannot but give the world poor and sick baby pigeons. Bring him here. Before I close, I must say that I am better. Bring Gay-Neck soon; the holy lama wishes to see you and him. Besides, all the five swifts have arrived this week from the south; they will surely divert your pet bird."

I took Ghond's advice. I put Gay-Neck in one cage and his wife in another, and set out for the north.

How different the hills were in the spring from the previous autumn! Owing to the exigencies that had arisen, my parents had opened their house in Dentam months earlier than usual. After settling down there towards the last week of April, I took Gay-Neck along with me and set out in the company of a Tibetan caravan of ponies for Singalila, leaving his wife behind, so that if he were able to fly again he would return to her—just the thing needed to cure him. She was to be the drawing-card.

He might do it, Ghond had hoped, in order to return and help her hatch the newly laid eggs, though the day after our departure my parents destroyed the eggs; for we did not want sick and degenerate children who would grow up to shame the name of Gay-Neck.

I carried my bird on my shoulder, where he perched all day. During the night we kept him safely locked up in his cage, which proved beneficial to him. Twelve hours of mountain air and light improved his body, yet not once did he make the effort to fly off my shoulder and return to his mate to help her hatch the eggs.

The Himalayas in the spring are unique. The ground glittered with white violets, interspersed with raspberries already ripening here and there in the hot moist gorges where the ferns were spreading their large arms as if to embrace the white hills lying like precious stones on the indigo-blue throat of the sky. Sometimes we passed through thick forests where stunted oaks, prodigious elms, deodars (cedars) and chestnuts grew in such numbers that their branches shut out all sunlight. Tree against tree, bough against bough, and roots struggling with roots fought for light and life. Below them in arboreal darkness many deer grazed on abundant tall grass and saplings, only to be devoured in their turn by tigers, leopards and panthers. Everywhere life grew in abundance, all the more intensifying the struggle for existence among birds, beasts and plants. Such is the self-contradictory nature of existence. Even insects were not free of it.

When we emerged from the forest darkness and beheld the open spaces, the hot tropical sunlight suddenly shot its diamond points of fire into our helpless eyes. The golden tremble of dragon-flies filled the air; butterflies, sparrows, robins, grouse, parrots, papias (Indian thrushes), jays and pea-cocks clamoured and courted from tree to tree and peak to higher peak.

Now in the open space between tea-gardens on one side of the road and pine-forests on our right, we strove and staggered up inclines almost as straight as knives. There the air was so rarefied that we could hardly breathe. Sounds and echoes travelled very far: even a whisper could not escape being overheard from a distance of yards, and men and beasts alike became silent. Save for the clatter of their hoofs the ponies as well as the men moved with a sense of reverence for the solitude and stillness that shut down upon us. Here the indigo-blue hollow of the sky remained untainted by clouds, and untroubled by any movement save the sighing flight of cranes going northwards, or the deep-toned plunge of an eagle into declivities nearby. Everything was cold, keen and quickening. Orchids burst out almost overnight and opened their purple eyes upon us; marigolds brimmed with morning dew, and in the lakes below, blue and white lotuses opened their petals to the bees.

Now we were near Singalila. The lamasery raised its head and beckoned us from the hillside. Its wing-shaped roof and ancient walls floated like a banner against the horizon. I was encouraged to quicken my pace, and another hour's time found me climbing the steep pathway of the monastery.

What a relief it was to be there among men who lived above the battle of our everyday life! It being noon, I went down with Ghond through a forest of balsam to the spring in which we bathed ourselves and gave Gay-Neck a thorough wash. After the bird had had his dinner in his cage, Ghond and I went to the dining-room where the lamas were waiting for us. The room looked like a colonnade of ebony whose capitals were decorated with dragons of gold. The teak-wood beams, grown quite dark through many centuries, were carved into broad clear lotus designs, as delicate as jasmine but as strong as metal. On the floor of red sandstone, orange-robed monks were seated in silent prayer, which was their grace before each meal. Ghond and I waited at the entrance of the dining-room until the prayer was concluded with the chanting in unison, like the Gregorian chant:

> "Budham mē sáránām
> Dhārmám mē sáránām
> Ōm Mani pádmē Ōm."

In wisdom that is the Buddha is our refuge
In religion is our refuge
In the jewel of Truth (shining in the lotus of life) is our
refuge.

Now I went forward and saluted the abbot, whose grave face wreathed with smiles as he blessed me. After I had saluted the rest of the lamas, Ghond and I took our seats at the table made up of a series of small wooden stools, which came up to our chests as we squatted on the floor. It was nice to sit on the cool floor after a very hot day's journey. Our meal was of lentil soup, fried potatoes and curried eggplants. Since Ghond and I were vegetarians, we did not eat the eggs that were served at the table. Our drink consisted of hot green tea.

After dinner, the abbot invited Ghond and me to take our siesta in his company, and we climbed with him up to the topmost cliff, which was like an eagle's eyrie, over which grew a clump of firs, where we found a hard bare cell, without a stick of furniture anywhere, which I had never seen before. After we had seated ourselves there, the holy man said: "Here in the monastery we have prayed to Infinite Compassion twice every day for the healing of the nations of earth. Yet the war goes on, infecting even birds and beasts with fear and hate. Diseases of the emotions spread faster than the ills of the body. Mankind is going to be so loaded with fear, hate, suspicion and malice that it will take a whole generation before a new set of people can be reared completely free from them."

Infinite sadness furrowed the lama's hitherto unwrinkled brow, and the corners of his mouth drooped from sheer fatigue. Though he lived above the battle in his eagle's eyrie, he felt the burden of men's sins more grievously than those who had plunged the world into war.

But he resumed smiling: "Let us discuss Gay-Neck and Ghond who are with us. If you wish your pigeon to wing the serenity of the sky again, you must meditate on infinite courage, as Ghond has been doing for himself these many days."

"How, my Lord?" I asked eagerly. The abbot's yellow face suffused with colour; no doubt he was embarrassed by the directness of my question, and I felt ashamed. Directness, like hurry, is very sordid.

As if he knew my feeling, the lama in order to put me at my ease said: "Every dawn and sunset, seat Gay-Neck on your shoulder and say to yourself: 'Infinite courage is in all life. Each being that lives and breathes is a reservoir of infinite courage. May I be pure enough to pour infinite courage into those whom I touch!' If you do that for a while, one day your heart, mind and soul will become pure through and through. That instant the power of your soul, now without fear, without hate, without suspicion, will enter the pigeon and make him free. He who purifies himself to the greatest extent can

put into the world the greatest spiritual force. Do
what I advise you twice a day. All our lamas will
help you. Let us see what comes of it!"

The lama, after a moment's silence, continued:
"You have been told by Ghond, who knows animals better than any other man, that our fear
frightens others so that they attack us. Your pigeon
is so frightened that he thinks the whole sky is going
to attack him. No leaf tumbles without frightening
him. Not a shadow falls without driving panic into
his soul. Yet what is causing him suffering is himself.

"At this very time the village below us—yes, you
can see it over there to the north-west—is suffering
from the same trouble as Gay-Neck. As it is the
season for animals to come north, all the frightened
inhabitants are going about with old matchlocks in
order to kill wild beasts, and behold, the beasts attack them now, though they never did so before!
Buffalo come and eat up their crops, and leopards
steal their goats. Today news was brought here that
a wild buffalo killed a man last night. Though I tell
them to purge their minds of fear through prayer
and meditation, they will not do it."

"Why, O blessed Teacher," asked Ghond, "do
you not permit me to go and rid them of these
beasts?"

"Not yet," replied the lama. "Though you are
healed of fear in your waking moments, yet your

dreams harbour the curse of fright. Let us pray and meditate a few days longer, and your soul will be purged of all such dross. Then after you are healed, if the villagers below are still hurt by the beasts, you may go and help them."

The Wisdom of the Lama

AFTER ABOUT THE tenth day of strict and most sincere meditation in the manner he had prescribed, the lama sent for Gay-Neck and myself. So with the pigeon between my hands, I climbed up to his cell. The lama's face, generally yellow, today looked brown and very powerful. A strange poise and power shone in his almond-shaped eyes. He took Gay-Neck in his hands, and said:

"May the north wind bring healing unto you,
　May the south wind bring healing unto you,
May the winds of east and west pour healing into you.
　　　　　Fear flees from you,
　　　　　Hate flees from you,
　　　And suspicion flees from you.

Courage like a rushing tide gallops through you;
Peace possesses your entire being,
And serenity and strength have become your two wings.
In your eyes shines courage;
Power and prowess dwell in your heart!
You are healed,
You are healed,
You are healed!
Peace,   peace,   peace."

We sat there meditating on those thoughts till the sun set, smiting the Himalayan peaks into multi-coloured flames. The valleys, the hollows and the woods about us put on a mantle of purple glory.

Slowly Gay-Neck hopped down from the lama's hands, walked out to the entrance of the cell and looked at the sunset. He opened his left wing, and waited. Then softly and ever so slowly he opened his right wing, feather by feather, muscle by muscle, until at last it spread out like a sail. Instead of doing anything theatrical such as instantly flying off, he carefully shut his two wings as if they were two precious but fragile fans. He too knew how to salute the sunset. With the dignity of a priest he walked downstairs, but hardly had he gone out of sight when I heard—I fancied I heard—the flapping of his wings. I was about to get up hastily and see what had really happened, but the holy man put his hand on my shoulder and restrained me while an inscrutable smile played on his lips.

The next morning I told Ghond what had happened. He replied tartly: "Gay-Neck opened his wings to salute the setting sun, you say. There is nothing surprising in that. Animals are religious, though man in his ignorance thinks they are not. I have seen monkeys, eagles, pigeons, leopards and even the mongoose adore the dawn and sunset."

"Can you show them to me?"

Ghond answered, "Yes. But not now; let us go and give Gay-Neck his breakfast."

When we reached his cage we found its door open—and no pigeon within. I was not surprised, for I had left the cage unlocked every night that we had been at the lamasery. But where had he gone? We could not find him in the main building, so we went to the library. There in a deserted outer cell we found some of his feathers, and nearby Ghond detected a weasel's footprints. That made us suspect trouble. But if the weasel had attacked and killed him, there would be blood on the floor. Then, whither had he fled? What had he done? Where was he now? We wandered for an hour. Just as we had decided to give up the search, we heard him cooing, and there he was on the roof of the library, talking to his old friends the Swifts, who were clinging to their nest under the eaves. We could make out their answer to his cooing. Mr. Swift said, "Cheep, cheep, cheep!" I cried to Gay-Neck in joy, and gave him his call to breakfast: "Aya—á—ay." He curved his

neck, and listened. Then, as I called again, he saw
me, and instantly flapped his wings loudly, then flew
down and sat on my wrist, as cool as a cucumber.
During the earliest dawn he must have heard the
priests' footsteps going up to their morning meditation, and got out of his cage, then gone astray to the
outer cell where no doubt a young and inexpert
weasel had attacked him. A veteran like Gay-Neck
could easily outwit the weasel by presenting him
with a few feathers only. While the young hopeful
was looking for the pigeon inside a lot of torn
feathers, his would-be victim flew up into the sky.
There he found his old friend Swift, flying to salute
the rising sun. And after they had performed their
morning worship together, they had come down for
a friendly chat on the roof of the monastery library.

That day very terrible news reached the lamasery. A wild buffalo had attacked the village that
the lama had spoken of the day before. He had
come there during the previous evening and killed
two people who were going home from a meeting
of the village elders that was held around the com-
munal threshing floor. The villagers had sent up a
deputation to the abbot to say a prayer for the destruction of the beast and begging him to exorcise
the soul out of the brute. The holy man said that he
would use means that would kill the murderous buffalo in twenty-four hours. "Go home in peace, O
beloved ones of Infinite Compassion. Your prayers

will be answered. Do not venture out of doors after nightfall. Stay home and meditate on peace and courage." Ghond, who was present, asked, "How long has this fellow been pestering your village?" The entire deputation affirmed that he had been coming every night for a week. He had eaten up almost half of their spring crop. Again begging for strong and effective incantation and exorcism to kill the buffalo, they went down to their village.

After the deputation had left, the lama said to Ghond, who was standing by, "O chosen one of victory, now that you are healed, go forth to slay the murderer."

"But, my Lord!"

"Fear no more, Ghond. Your meditations have healed you. Now test in the woods what you have acquired here by this means. In solitude men gain power and poise that they must test in the multitude. Ere the sun sets twice from now, you shall return victorious. As an earnest of my perfect faith in your success, I request you to take this boy and his pigeon with you. Surely I would not ask you to take a boy of sixteen with you if I doubted your powers or the outcome of your mission. Go, bring the murderer to justice."

That afternoon we set out for the jungle. I was overjoyed at the prospect of spending at least one night in there again. What a pleasure it was to go with Ghond and the pigeon, both whole and well once more, in quest of a wild buffalo! Is there any boy on earth who would not welcome such an opportunity?

So, thoroughly equipped with rope ladders, a lassoo and knives, with Gay-Neck on my shoulder, we set out. The British Government forbids the use of firearms to the common people of India, and so we carried no rifles.

About three in the afternoon we reached the village north-west of the lamasery. There we took up the trail of the buffalo. We followed it through dense woods and wide clearings. Here and there we crossed a brook or had to climb over mammoth fallen trees. It was extraordinary how clear the buffalo's hoof-prints were, and how deep!

Ghond remarked: "He must have been frightened to death, for see how heavily he has trodden here. Animals in their normal unafraid state leave very little trace behind, but when frightened, they act as if the terror of being killed weighed their bodies down. This fellow's hoofs have made prodigious and clear marks wherever he went. How frightened he must have been!"

At last we reached an impassable river. Its current, according to Ghond, was sharp enough to break our legs had we stepped into it. Strangely enough, the buffalo too had not dared to cross it. So we followed his precedent, looking for more hoof-prints on the bank. In twenty more minutes we found that they swerved off the stream-bank and disappeared into a thick jungle that looked as black as a pit, although it was hardly five in the afternoon. This place could not have been more than half an hour's run from the village, for a wild buffalo of any age.

Ghond asked, "Do you hear the song of the water?" After listening for several minutes I heard the sound of water kissing the sedges, and other grass not far off, with gurgling groaning sounds. We were about twenty feet from a lake into which the river ran. "The murderous buffalo is hiding—probably asleep somewhere between here and the lagoon," cried Ghond. "Let us make our home on one of the twin trees yonder. It is getting dark, and I am sure he will be here soon. We should not be found on the floor of the jungle when he turns up. There is hardly a space of four feet between the trees!"

His last words struck me as curious. So I examined the space between the trees. They were tall and massive, and between them lay a piece of earth just broad enough to afford room for both of us walking abreast of each other.

"Now I shall lay down my fear-soaked tunic halfway between these Twins." Then Ghond proceeded to take from under his tunic a bundle of old clothes that he had been wearing until today. He placed them on the ground, then climbed one of the trees. After Ghond had gone up, he swung down a rope

ladder for me. I climbed up on it with Gay-Neck
fluttering and beating his wings on my shoulders in
order to keep his balance. Both of us safely reached
the branch on which Ghond was sitting, and since
the evening was coming on apace, we sat still for a
while.

The first thing I noticed as the dusk fell was bird-
life. Herons, hornbills, grouse, pheasant, song-sparrows and emerald flocks of parrots seemed to infest
the forest. The drone of the bee, the cut-cut-cut of
the woodpecker and the shrill cry of the eagle far
overhead blended with the tearing, crying noises of
the mountain torrent and the staccato laughter of
the already waking hyenas.

The tree on which we made our home for the
night was very tall. We went farther up in order to
make sure that no leopard or serpent was above
us. After a close inspection we chose a couple of
branches between which we hung our rope ladder
in the shape of a strong hammock. Just as we had
made ourselves secure on our perch, Ghond pointed
to the sky. I looked up at once. There floated on
wings of ruby a very large eagle. Though darkness
was rising like a flood from the floor of the jungle,
in the spaces above the sky burned "like a pigeon's
throat," and through it circled again and again that
solitary eagle who was no doubt, according to
Ghond, performing his worship of the setting sun.
His presence had already had a stilling effect on the

birds and insects of the forest. Though he was far above them, yet like a congregation of mute worshippers, they kept silent while he, their King, flew backwards and forwards, and vaulted before their God, the Father of Light, with the ecstasy of a hierophant. Slowly the ruby fire ebbed from his wings. Now they became purple sails fringed with sparks of gold. As if his adoration was at last concluded, he rose higher and, as an act of self-immolation before his deity, flew towards the flaming peaks burning with fire, and vanished in their splendour like a moth.

Below, a buffalo's bellowing unlocked the insect voices one by one, tearing into shreds and tatters the stillness of the evening. An owl hooted near by, making Gay-Neck snuggle closely to my heart under my tunic. Suddenly the Himalayan Doël, a nightbird, very much like a nightingale, flung abroad its magic song. Like a silver flute blown by a God, trill upon trill, cadenza upon cadenza, spilled its torrential peace that rushed like rain down the boughs of the trees, dripping over their rude barks to the floor of the jungle, then through their very roots into the heart of the earth.

The enchantment of an early summer night in the Himalayas will remain for ever indescribable. In fact it was so sweet and lonely that I felt very sleepy. Ghond put an extra rope around me that held me secure to the trunk of the tree. Then I put my head on his shoulder in order to sleep comfortably. But before I did so, he told me of his plan:

"Those cast-off garments of mine are what I wore while my heart was possessed of fear. They have a strange odour. If that brother-in-law (idiot) of a buffalo gets their scent, he will come hither. He who is frightened responds to the odour of fear. If he comes to investigate my cast-off dress, we shall do what we can to him. I hope we can lassoo and take him home as tame as a heifer. . . ." I did not hear the rest of his words, for I had fallen asleep.

I do not know how long I slept, but suddenly I was roused by a terrific bellowing. When I opened my eyes, Ghond, who was already awake, undid the rope around me and pointed below. In the faint light of the dawn at first I saw nothing, but I heard distinctly the groaning and grunting of an angry beast. In the tropics the day breaks rapidly. I looked down most intently. Now in the growing light of day I saw. . . . There could be no two opinions about what I saw. Yes, there was a hillock of shining jet rubbing its dark side against the tree on which we sat. It was about ten feet long, I surmised, though half of its bulk was covered by the leaves and boughs of the trees. The beast looked like a black opal coming out of a green furnace, such was the glitter of the newly grown foliage under the morning sun. I thought, "The buffalo that in nature looks healthy and silken, in a zoo is a mangy creature with matted mane and dirty skin. Can those who see buffalo in captivity ever conceive how beautiful they can be? What a pity that most young people instead of seeing one animal in nature—which is worth a hundred in any zoo—must derive their knowledge of God's creatures from their appearance in prisons! If we cannot perceive any right proportion of man's moral nature by looking at prisoners in a jail, how do we manage to think that we know all about an animal by gazing at him penned in a cage?"

However, to return to that murderous buffalo at the foot of our tree. Gay-Neck was freed from under my tunic and left to roam on the tree, which Ghond and I descended by a number of branches, like the rungs of a ladder, till we reached a branch that was about two feet above the buffalo. He did not see us. Ghond swiftly tied around the tree-trunk one end of the long lassoo. I noticed that the buffalo was playing underneath by putting his horns now and then through a tattered garment, what was left of Ghond's clothes. No doubt the odour of man in them had attracted him. Though his horns were clean, there were marks of fresh blood on his head. Apparently he had gone to the village and killed another person during the night. That roused Ghond. He whispered into my ear: "We shall get him alive. You slip this lassoo over his horns from above." In a trice Ghond had leaped off the branch near the rear of the buffalo. That startled the beast. But he could not turn round, for close to his right was a tree that I mentioned before, and to his left was the tree on which I stood. He had to go back or forward between the twins in order to get out from them, but before this happened I had flung the lassoo over his head. The touch of the rope acted like electricity upon him. He hastened backwards, in order to slip off the lassoo, so fast that Ghond, had he not already gone around the next tree, would have been trampled and cut to death by the sharp hoofs of the beast. But now, to my utter consternation, I noticed that instead of gripping his two horns at the very root, I had succeeded in lassooing only one of them. That instant I shrieked to Ghond in terror: "Beware! only one of his horns is caught. The rope may slip off that one any time. Run! Run up a tree."

But that intrepid hunter ignored my advice. Instead he stood facing the enemy a short distance away from him. Then I saw the brute lower his head and plunge forward. I shut my eyes in terror.

When I opened them again, I saw that the bull was tugging at the rope that held him by the horn and kept him from butting into the tree behind which Ghond stood. His monstrous bellowing filled the jungle with a fearful racket. Echoes of it coursed one after another like frightened shrieking children.

Since the bull had not yet succeeded in reaching him, Ghond drew his razor-sharp dagger, about a foot and a half long and two inches broad. He slowly slipped behind another tree to the right, then vanished out of sight. The bull just ran straight at the spot where he had seen Ghond last. Fortunately, the rope was still clinging tightly to his horn.

Here Ghond changed his tactics. He ran away in the opposite direction, zigzagging in between different trees. This he did to go where his odour could not reach the bull, blown down to him by the wind. But though he was bewildered, yet the bull turned and followed. He again saw the bundle of Ghond's clothes on the ground under our tree. That maddened him. He sniffed, and then worried it with his horns.

By now Ghond was down wind. Though I could not see him, I surmised that he could tell by the odour where the bull was in case the trees hid him from view. The beast bellowed again, as he put his horns through Ghond's clothes, which raised a terrific tumult in the trees all around. From nowhere came flocks of monkeys running from branch to branch. Squirrels ran like rats from trees to the jungle-floor, then back again. Swarms of birds, such as jays, herons and parrots, were flying about and shrieking in unison with crows, owls and kites. Suddenly the bull charged again. I saw that Ghond was standing there calmly facing him. If ever I saw a man as calm as calmness itself, it was Ghond. The bull's hind legs throbbed and swept on like swords. Then something happened. He reared in the air; no doubt it was the pull of the lassoo rope, of which one end was tied to our tree. He rose several feet above the ground, then fell. That instant, like a dry twig snapped by a child, his horn cracked and flew up in the air. The breaking created an irresistible momentum that flung him sideways on the ground. He almost rolled over, his legs kicking the air violently. Instantly Ghond leaped forward like a spark from the flint. Seeing him, the buffalo balanced himself and sat on his haunches, snorting. He almost succeeded in rising to his feet, but Ghond struck near his shoulder with the dagger. Its deadly edge dug deep, and Ghond pressed on it with his entire weight. A bellow like a volcanic eruption shook the jungle, and with it a fountain of liquid ruby spurted up. Unable to bear the sight any longer, I again shut my eyes.

In a few minutes, when I came down from my perch, I found that the buffalo had died of a haemorrhage. It lay in a deep pool of blood. And near by sat Ghond on the ground, wiping himself from the stain of his encounter. I knew that he wished to be left alone. So I went to the old tree and called to Gay-Neck. He made no response. I went all the way up to the topmost branch of the tree. But in vain—he was not there.

When I came down, Ghond had cleansed himself. He pointed at the sky. We beheld nature's scavengers. Kites below, and far above them vultures flew.

They had already learned that someone had died and they must clean up the jungle.

Ghond said: "We shall find the pigeon in the monastery. He flew with the rest of the birds, doubtless. Let us depart hence soon." But before starting homeward. I went to measure the dead buffalo, to whom flies had been swarming from every direction. He was ten feet and a half in length, and his forelegs measured over three feet.

Our trudge back towards the monastery was made in silence that was broken only when, about noonday, we had reached the stricken village and informed its headman that their enemy was dead. He was relieved to hear of it, though he was very sad because during the previous evening the buffalo had killed his aged mother, who was going to the village temple to her worship before sunset.

We were very hungry and walked fast, and soon we reached the monastery. At once I made inquiries about my pigeon. Gay-Neck was not there! It was terrible. But the old holy man said, as we chatted in his cell, "He is safe as are you, Ghond." After a pause of several minutes he asked, "What is troubling your peace of mind?"

The old hunter thought out quietly what he was going to say. "Nothing, my Lord, save this: I hate to kill anything. I wanted to catch that bull alive, and alas! I had to destroy him. When that horn of his broke, and there was nothing between him and me, I had to put my knife through a vital vein. I am so sorry I could not get him alive in order to sell him to a zoo."

"O you soul of commercialism!" I exclaimed. "I am not sorry that the bull died. Better death than to be caged for the rest of his life in a zoo. Real death is preferable to living death."

"If you had only slipped the lassoo over both horns!" Ghond retorted.

The holy one ejaculated, "Both of you should be concerned about Gay-Neck, not about what is already dead."

Ghond said, "True. Let us search for him on the morrow."

But the holy one replied: "No. Return to Dentam, my son. Your family is anxious about you. I hear their thoughts."

The next day we left for Dentam on a pair of ponies. By forced march and changing ponies twice a day at different posts, we reached Dentam in three days' time. As we were going up towards our house, we encountered a very excited servant of my family. He said that Gay-Neck had returned three days ago. But since we had not come back with him, my parents had begun to worry, and they had sent out parties searching after us, alive or dead.

He and I almost ran up to the house. In another ten minutes my mother's arms were around me, and Gay-Neck, with his feet on my head, was fluttering his wings in order to balance himself.

I cannot begin to describe how overjoyed I was to hear that Gay-Neck had flown at last. He had winged all the way from the lamasery to our home in Dentam. He had not faltered or failed! "O thou soul of flight, thou pearl among pigeons," I exclaimed to myself as Ghond and I accelerated our steps.

Thus ended our pilgrimage to Singalila. It healed both Gay-Neck and Ghond of the disease of fear and hate that they had caught on the battle-fields. No labor would be in vain if it could heal a single soul of these worst ills of life.

Instead of spinning out a sermon at the end of this story, let me say this:

"Whatever we think and feel will colour what we say or do. He who fears, even unconsciously, or has his least little dream tainted with hate, will inevitably, sooner or later, translate these two qualities into his action. Therefore, my brothers, live courage, breathe courage and give courage. Think and feel love so that you will be able to pour out of yourselves peace and serenity as naturally as a flower gives forth fragrance.

"Peace be unto all!"